The Anniversary

A QUICK READS COLLECTION

Fanny Blake
Elizabeth Buchan
Rowan Coleman
Jenny Colgan
Philippa Gregory
Matt Haig
Veronica Henry
Andy McNab
Richard Madeley
John O'Farrell
and
The Hairy Bikers

Fanny Blake was a publisher for many years, editing both fiction and non-fiction before becoming a freelance journalist and writer. She has written five novels including *With a Friend Like You* and *House of Dreams*, as well as a previous Quick Read title, *Red for Revenge*. She is also Books Editor of *Woman & Home* magazine.

Elizabeth Buchan's previous novels include *Light of the Moon*, the prizewinning *Consider the Lily*, the *New York Times* bestseller *Revenge of the Middle-Aged Woman*, and her most recent book *I Can't Begin to Tell You*. As well as her novels, Elizabeth's short stories have been broadcast on BBC Radio 4 and published in a range of magazines.

Rowan Coleman lives with her husband and five children in a very full house in Hertfordshire. Despite being dyslexic, Rowan loves writing and has written twelve novels, including the *Sunday Times* Bestseller *The Memory Book*, *The Accidental Mother* and the award-winning *Runaway Wife*. Her latest novel is *We Are All Made of Stars*.

Jenny Colgan is the author of numerous bestselling novels in the romantic comedy and sci-fi genres, including *Christmas at the Cupcake Café* and *The Loveliest Chocolate Shop in Paris*. Her latest novel, *Little Beach Street Bakery*, is a *Sunday Times* Top Ten bestseller, and she also writes extensively for *Doctor Who*. Jenny is married with three children and lives near Edinburgh.

Philippa Gregory was an established historian and writer when she discovered her interest in the Tudor period and wrote the internationally bestselling novel *The Other Boleyn Girl*. She has written several historical novels including most recently *The Taming of the Queen*, a *Sunday Times* Number One bestseller. She lives with her family on a small farm in Yorkshire.

Matt Haig has written several novels including his bestselling debut *The Last Family in England*, *The Radleys* and *The Humans*. He is also the author of the award-winning children's novel *Shadow Forest*, and it's sequel, *The Runaway Troll*, as well as *A Boy Called Christmas*. His most recent book, *Reasons to Stay Alive,* is a non-fiction bestseller. He lives in Brighton with the writer Andrea Semple and their two children.

Veronica Henry was a scriptwriter for *The Archers*, *Heartbeat* and *Holby City* before turning to writing novels. Her bestsellers include *The Beach Hut* and *A Night on the Orient Express*, which won

Romantic Novel of the Year 2014. Her latest novel is *High Tide.*

Andy McNab was abandoned as a baby so his start in life was tough. He was recruited into the Army from juvenile detention at the age of sixteen. The next six months in the Army education system changed the course of his life for ever. During the Gulf War he commanded Bravo Two Zero, and was the British Army's most highly decorated serving soldier when he finally left the SAS in February 1993. He wrote about his experiences in the massive bestseller *Bravo Two Zero* and is also the author of both the bestselling Nick Stone and Tom Buckingham thriller series. He has written three previous Quick Read titles, *The Grey Man*, *Last Night Another Soldier* and *Today Everything Changes.*

Richard Madeley was born in 1956. He worked on local newspapers before moving to BBC local radio. He met Judy Finnigan when they both presented the nightly news programme on Granada TV in Manchester. They launched ITV's *This Morning* in 1988 and after thirteen years took their now famous TV show to Channel 4. It ran for seven years and was a huge success, launching the still-active Richard and Judy Book Club.

Richard is the bestselling author of two novels, *Some Day I'll Find You* and *The Way You Look Tonight*, and is about to complete his third.

John O'Farrell is the bestselling author of the novels *The Best a Man Can Get, This is Your Life, May Contain Nuts, The Man Who Forgot His Wife* and his latest: *There's Only Two David Beckhams* – a football fantasy set at the World Cup in Qatar 2020. His non-fiction work includes *An Utterly Impartial History of Britain* and *Things Can Only Get Better*. His work has been translated into over twenty-five languages and adapted for TV and radio. Other writing credits include *Spitting Image, Have I Got News for You, Chicken Run* and the Broadway musical *Something Rotten!*

The Hairy Bikers, Si King and Dave Myers, have been cooking together for more than twenty years. They have appeared in over twenty series including *Mums Know Best, Bakeation, Meals on Wheels* and most recently, *Northern Exposure*. The Hairy Bikers have written sixteen books to date, including *Perfect Pies, Great Curries, The Hairy Dieters: How to love food and lose weight* and *Meat Feasts*.

First published in Great Britain in 2016
by Orion Books
an imprint of the Orion Publishing Group Ltd

An Hachette UK company

10 9 8 7 6 5 4 3 2 1

Song titles taken from the following copyright claimants:
Love Me Tender written by Elvis Presley & Vera Matson (Twentieth Century Music Corporation PWH) 1956
Hound Dog written by Jerry Leiber & Mike Stoller 1956
All Shook Up written by Otis Blackwell and Elvis Presley 1957
Suspicious Minds written by Mark James, pseud. of Fred Zambon 1968

ISBN 978 1 4091 5907 0

Typeset at The Spartan Press Ltd, Lymington, Hants

Printed and bound in Great Britain by Clays Ltd, St Ives plc

The Orion Publishing Group's policy is to use papers that are natural, renewable and recyclable products and made from wood grown in sustainable forests. The logging and manufacturing processes are expected to conform to the environmental regulations of the country of origin.

The Orion Publishing Group Ltd
Carmelite House, 50 Victoria Embankment
London EC4Y 0DZ

www.orionbooks.co.uk

The Anniversary

Edited by Veronica Henry

The Other Half

Fanny Blake

Josie turned off her car engine. Mr and Mrs Warren knew she was waiting. Someone had waved at her from a window when she had arrived. She picked up her paper from the passenger seat, then put it down and looked back at the house.

Behind the black railings was a small but smart front garden with neat box hedges circling a tree covered in large pink flowers. Josie had no idea what the tree was. You didn't get trees like that on the housing estate where she lived with her mum and her two girls, Kelly and Daisy.

The front gate opened onto a paved path that led to a porch supported by tall fluted columns and a shiny black front door. Through the window she could see a huge gilt-framed mirror over a marble fireplace and a chandelier hanging from the ceiling. Someone drew first one then the other curtain, shutting her out of the better life she dreamed of. She switched on the radio.

1

Humming along to Adele's 'Someone Like You', Josie tapped out the beat on the wheel. She wasn't used to this waiting. As the only female working for the minicab firm, she was usually given the single women or children who were almost always ready when she arrived. But tonight the Warrens' usual driver was held up in traffic so Brendan, the controller, had given her the job. Brendan always made a point of looking out for her, and the Warrens were valuable customers, so she was happy to sit tight.

Her deep-blue Vauxhall car was her pride and joy. It was the one thing her husband had left her when he ran off with her best friend. That and their two girls. This was her haven, the only place where she had any private time away from the cramped little house the three of them shared with her mum.

Josie looked at her watch. Twenty minutes late. Perhaps they hadn't seen her after all? Should she ring the doorbell? No, Brendan would have let her know if she needed to do that. At that moment, the front door swung open. A creamy hallway was bathed in a soft light.

As she got out of the car, there was a shout. 'Isabel! We must go!' Into view came a man in a dinner jacket: a dead ringer for George Clooney. If that was Mr Warren, what would Mrs Warren be like? Josie glanced down at her worn pink fleece, her jeans that had got so much tighter since she started this job, her old trainers.

Mrs Warren was tall and slim, wearing a long figure-hugging dress in pale blue with sparkles on the bodice. You couldn't get anything like that in the shops Josie could afford. Over her shoulder was a white fur wrap. Josie wondered if it was real. She wouldn't be surprised. The two of them looked like film stars, and they were getting into her car. Thank God she had cleaned it that morning. There was not a trace of her toast-eating, carton-drinking girls she had dropped off at school.

Josie held open the rear door for Mrs Warren, breathing in the scent of roses that came with her. And with that came another smell: the smell of money, success, privilege and, no doubt, children who wanted for nothing. That was the sort of life that Josie could get used to.

After shutting Mrs Warren's door, Josie raced round to open Mr Warren's. He flicked at a bit of imaginary dirt on the seat, then bent his head so the slicked-back greying hair didn't touch the door frame as he climbed in. Neither of them said a word to her.

They had fastened their seat belts by the time Josie was back behind the wheel.

'The Ritz.' Mr Warren gave the simple command. No 'please', Josie noticed.

'The air freshener's very strong.' His wife spoke in a stage whisper. She obviously disliked the smell.

Josie cleared her throat. She had taken some time selecting the Lemon Zinger from the range of air fresheners at the garage. She was always careful to choose a scent she liked, because she spent so much time in the car. She started the engine. At the end of the road, she waited for a gap in the traffic.

'We're in a hurry,' said Mrs Warren. Her voice was like broken glass. 'So make sure you take the quickest route.'

'Of course,' said Josie, wishing she could point out that they'd be in less of a hurry if they had come out when she had arrived. But they were customers, so she had to watch her tongue. She turned into the main road.

'I don't know why we have to spend our anniversary entertaining your clients.' Mrs Warren said to her husband.

He heaved a sigh. 'You know exactly why, darling.'

Josie watched him straighten his bow tie in her rear-view mirror.

'We can't afford to lose the business. And we mustn't be late.'

Josie thought that last remark might have been directed at her but she couldn't be sure.

'And why the Ritz?' his wife wondered. 'Anyone and everyone goes there these days. Doesn't matter who you are.'

And what was wrong with 'anyone', Josie thought? Life might have given the rich a different start and other opportunities, but underneath they were just the same as 'anyone' else.

Mr Warren gave a short laugh. 'I've never thought about it before but you're quite right. At least it's only for one evening. By the way, did you talk to the children?'

'About them having to pay for their own flights from Thailand? We agreed you'd do that.'

'That's not what we said at all.' Mr Warren's voice was tight with anger. 'But perhaps now's not the best moment to discuss it.'

Josie saw him nod in her direction. In which case, why bring it up in the first place, she wondered.

'We only ever discuss things when it suits you.'

Could Mrs Warren hear how bitter and resentful she sounded?

'Be quiet, Isabel. Not now.'

The traffic ground to a halt. There was a strained silence in the back seat .

'This isn't the route I'd have taken.' Mrs Warren spoke under her breath but Josie heard every word. She tightened her grip on the wheel.

Through the static on the intercom, Josie heard the minicab controller Brendan giving her call sign. 'When you finish, head to the Coach and Horses.' He gave her the client's name and the address of the pub, then signed off.

The traffic was moving again. Josie let her thoughts wander to Brendan. He had been good to her, taking her on as a driver so soon after Bill had walked out on her and the children for good. Exactly a year ago, in fact. As a newly single mother, Josie had badly needed work but had nothing much going for her except her driving licence. This job gave her the freedom she needed, and a woman driver was an asset to Brendan and his minicab firm.

So the arrangement had worked both ways. And she liked him. It had even crossed her mind that one day they might get to know each other better. But she would never be the one to make the first move. Not this soon after her husband Bill leaving her, anyway. Underneath the Lemon Zinger scent in the car, she caught the trace of Mrs Warren's perfume.

'Is this really the best way?' Mr Warren's voice jolted Josie out of her dream. The traffic had slowed down to a crawl again.

She glanced in the mirror to find his steely eyes staring back at her.

'Which way would you like me to go, sir?' she asked.

'I'm sure it would be quicker if we went through Regent's Park.' Mrs Warren chipped in.

'Regent's Park's closed tonight,' Josie said, and swung down a side street, taking one of the rat runs that the black cabs used. Mrs Warren grabbed the seat to steady herself. Josie allowed herself a smile as she went a little too fast over a traffic control bump.

They emerged into another stream of traffic. A white van blared its horn and slid in front of them.

Mrs Warren gasped. 'That was close.'

It hadn't been close at all. Josie had seen the van and slowed to let it by. She took a deep breath.

'It's quarter to eight,' pointed out Mr Warren.

The digital clock meant Josie could see exactly what the time was and how much longer she would have to put up with Mr and Mrs Warren. For all they cared, she could have been a robot behind the wheel. After all, she was just the 'anyone and everyone' they so despised. She used all the shortcuts and dodges she knew, pulling up outside the hotel at one minute to eight.

'Ben, have you got any cash for a tip?' Mrs Warren dug into her glittery bag that was barely big enough for a lipstick. But Mr Warren was already halfway up the steps and didn't look back. 'You'll pick us up at eleven?' Mrs Warren pressed the exact fare into Josie's hand.

'If I'm given the job of picking you up, I will, but I don't know where I'll be.' Josie hoped never to see them again, but that was up to Brendan. She watched Mrs Warren glide into the hotel after her husband. Classy she might be, but she was cold as ice.

Josie thought of her own family. They might not have much – but at least they knew how to treat people.

Back in the car, feeling cross, Josie called Brendan to say she was on her way back. He insisted she check in after every job.

'How did that one go?' he asked, his warm Irish accent returning her to the world she knew.

She hesitated.

'Awkward? That's why I've never given them to you before. Jim will pick them up later.'

'Thanks. That'd be great.' She didn't need

to say more. She heard a rustle of paper, then Brendan spoke again.

'You're on your way to the next job?'

'I'll be there on time, don't worry.'

'Ah, sure I'm not worrying.' He laughed. 'We'll speak later.'

The traffic back was better so she got to the Coach and Horses in good time. Leaving the Warrens behind her had lifted her mood. A few smokers stood outside the pub but no one looked at the car. She got out, locked up and pushed open the door to be greeted by a beery warmth and the buzz of voices. She walked over to the bar to wait while the tattooed barman served up a pint.

'Won't be a minute, love.' He winked.

'Josie!'

She turned at the sound of her name. At a table in the corner sat Brendan, smart, in a jacket for once. In front of him stood a pint and a glass of white wine. So he was spoken for. Her disappointment took her by surprise. He stood up and waved her over.

'Sit down.' He pulled out the other chair for her.

'Me? But I'm here for my next fare, remember?' She looked around the crowded pub. 'Where's your other...?'

Brendan was smiling. 'This is for you.' He handed her the wine. 'I didn't think you'd come if I asked. We're knocking off work now, you and me. We're going to celebrate you being one of our drivers for a year to the day.'

She felt a grin spread across her face as she took her seat. Brendan didn't seem to care about her fleece, or notice her tighter jeans. He was watching her with a twinkle in his eye. It turned out that what she had always imagined to be a 'better' life was not what she wanted for herself and her family at all. This was where she belonged. She raised her glass.

Who needed the Ritz?

Moment of Glory

Elizabeth Buchan

On a June morning in 1954, Ellen is doing the chores in her kitchen. The radio is on but she is feeling annoyed with the heat and the effort. The oven is the very devil to get clean and the floor requires two lots of red polish before it looks halfway decent.

In an effort to cool down, she plunges her hands into the sink full of cold water.

Standing there, enjoying the sweet relief, she looks through the window to the street. Her eight-year-old son, Sam, is playing hopscotch with his best friend, Mike. Mike is winning and Sam looks cross. Ellen smiles at the sight. Sam is not a good loser.

Feeling better, Ellen dries her hands on the towel. They are sore from scrubbing the laundry earlier. Her knuckles are bright red from the soda she added to the water to whiten the sheets.

She peers into the mirror propped up on the windowsill by the sink and her irritation returns.

Ellen is not looking her best. Scraped back with an old bit of ribbon, her hair needs a wash. Plus, it would help matters if she put on some lipstick.

Crossly, she unties the hair ribbon. Her hair falls down over her shoulders and she combs her fingers through it. *That's better*, she thinks.

The pips for the news sound on the radio. An announcer says, 'This is the twelve o'clock news for the 6th of June'.

She feels her throat tighten. The 6th of June is a date which brings back memories which mean everything to her. Exciting, never-to-be forgotten memories.

Ellen discovers that she is staring at herself in the mirror so hard that her eyes begin to water. She rubs them and takes another look.

What she sees makes her heart jump.

The face looking back at her has changed. It is younger and softer, with curly hair and scarlet lipstick.

Is she going mad? Is she ill? Is it possible that what she is seeing in the mirror is the face that was hers ten years ago . . . ?

In 1943 – in the middle of World War II – nineteen-year-old Ellen was chosen to work as a signals clerk in the top-secret Station 53.

Her job was to listen to the radio messages

from the far-off battlefields and to note them down. 'Do it how you like,' said the instructor, 'but you get these messages down correctly. No mistakes. No making anything up. Otherwise, you put lives in danger. Do you understand me?'

Ellen nodded.

The instructor placed a piece of paper in front of her. On it was written: XUPTR WRBNT. 'What's this?'

'A message in code?'

'Correct. This is how the messages will come in. Why are they sent in code?'

'So they cannot be read if the enemy gets hold of them.'

'Correct.'

Ellen was also made to sign the Official Secrets Act which made her promise that she would never utter a word about her job.

The officer who gave her the papers to sign set it out in great detail. 'You are never to talk about what you do. Not to your parents, your brothers and sisters, your friends, or your boyfriend. If you do, you will face a prison sentence.'

She had signed willingly but there were times when she found it hard to say nothing. Jack, her boyfriend in the Navy, asked a lot of questions and refused to shut up until he was sent away to sea. Meg, her sister, was just as bad.

'Why can't you tell us what you do, Ellen?' She fixed her big eyes on Ellen. 'Go on. Tell us. I can keep a secret. *Please*.'

There were not many things in life of which Ellen was sure. Except for one. Her sister was unable to keep a secret. Ever.

But she, Ellen, could keep a secret. And did. During her time at Station 53, she never said a word about her work and she was proud of herself.

Over the months which followed, Ellen learned many things and perfected her skills. She learned that the radio signal was sometimes weak and it could be difficult to understand the Morse code messages. She had no idea who sent them or from where they were sent. But something strange happened. Ellen found that she began to develop a knack of understanding how the sender was feeling or what he or she was doing. She could tell this from the way they tapped out the letters.

They could be in a hurry. Or, under enemy fire. Or, angry. Or, very frightened.

Please stay safe, she sometimes prayed if she felt that the sender was in trouble.

It was hard work. By the end of each shift, Ellen and her fellow signals clerks were always exhausted. Even so, on some nights, she found it hard to sleep because she was worried she had let a mistake creep through into her work.

All of them at Station 53 knew that, if the job was only a tiny part of a very big war against Hitler, it was an important one. She and her friends talked about it over cups of tea in the station canteen. 'The bosses couldn't do without us,' one or other of them always ended up saying. Or, something like that.

The idea boosted them and kept them going through the grim and dark days.

On that morning of 6 June 1944, Ellen was coming to the end of an eight-hour shift. None of them had had anything to eat or drink. *Lord,* she thought. *I want the biggest cup of tea to drink, and the biggest bun to eat. I want to sleep for ever.*

Taking off her headphones, she dropped her head into her hands and pressed them against her tired eyes. Little flashes of light danced across them.

'When will this war end?' she muttered.

She thought of all things she would love to do. Go dancing. Be taken by Jack for a fancy meal in a restaurant. Eat an orange. Better still, eat a banana. Marry Jack when he came home and have his baby.

Above all, she longed for peace.

15

She longed for blue sky with no bombers flying across it.

She longed for pretty clothes and plenty of butter.

Her friend, Mary, who was sitting beside her, leant over and said: 'Cheer up, girl, you're not dead yet.'

Ellen lifted her head. 'Do I look as bad as I feel?'

'Worse.'

Ellen glanced at the clock on the wall and exclaimed, 'My God, the shift hasn't ended. Why didn't you say something?'

Frantic, she crammed on her headphones. Could she have missed a last-minute message coming through? That would be terrible, and it was the thing Ellen feared most. Not only that, but if she was ever found out, her good work record would be ruined.

Perfectly normal static sounds hissed in Ellen's ears which meant no messages were being transmitted. Her alarm died away, and she felt better.

The wireless set in front of Ellen had two dials, one of which showed the frequencies on which the radio signals were sent.

Her pencil was in her right hand ready to write down any of those last-minute messages. With her left hand, she adjusted the dial and checked the frequencies. Nothing. That was good. Finally, she twisted the needle until it hit the last frequency which she was due to check.

Contact!

Almost immediately, a stream of Morse code filled her ears and she began to take down the letters.

Dot. Dash. Dot. Dot. The letter 'L'.

Dash. Dash. Dash. 'O'.

Then 'N' and 'G'.

There was a pause. Ellen gripped the pencil tighter. Again, the Morse messages streamed into her headphones.

The letters, 'L' , 'I', 'V' and 'E'.

The letters kept coming.

She squinted down at her notepad. Something struck her as strange. Something was different.

When she realised what it was, she gasped.

'You all right, Ellen?' Mary looked up from her work.

Was she hearing correctly? Ellen was confused.

Her pencil finally came to a halt. It was then Ellen understood. The message which she was writing down was not in code. Instead, what she was reading on her notepad was what the signals clerks called 'in clear'.

LONG LIVE FRANCE
LONG LIVE BRITAIN
LONG LIVE THE ALLIES

Ellen was holding the pencil so tightly that her knuckles had turned white. Could it be? Had the invasion of France by the British and American troops begun? Was this D-Day which they had all so longed for?

An amazing thought struck her. If it *was* D-Day then she, Ellen, a small cog in the machine, was one of the first people to know.

She glanced around at the heads bent over their work. If the landings in France were happening, the end of the war might be in sight.

For a second or two, she allowed herself to think of all the glorious things that peace would bring. Butter and blue skies. Marriage and babies. Bananas and oranges. It would mean the end of death and hatred.

Tearing off her headphones, Ellen leapt to her feet. 'Listen . . .' she shouted. 'I think our boys have gone into France. I think the end of the war is coming.'

The cheer that went up in the signals room could have been heard for miles. Every single one of them in that room yelled and screamed, and one or two danced on the spot.

Ellen climbed up onto her chair and waved the message in the air. 'Long live France. Long live Britain. Long live the Allies . . .'

She was weeping with joy.

Ah, her memories.

Her wonderful memories of that sweet, sweet moment when she stood on a chair, dizzy with excitement and crying her heart out.

Ten years on, peace is not quite as Ellen imagined. Yes, she eats bananas. Yes, she is married to Jack. Yes, she has a small block of butter ready for hot buttered toast at Sunday tea.

But being a wife and mother is hard work and, sometimes, boring. There is no office gossip. No listening for messages. No dancing on the spot.

Instead, she is scrubbing, cleaning and cooking.

'Mum,' says a voice from the doorway. 'Why are you staring in the mirror?'

Sam, her son, has come inside. She turns around and looks at him. Small, fair-haired, with a front tooth missing – she loves him more than she can possibly say.

'Mum?'

'I was remembering when something very special happened to me during the war.'

Sam looks thoughtful. 'Aren't I special?'

Ellen relives those amazing scenes at Station 53. How the signals clerks had cheered and made her tea with a spoonful of precious sugar. Everyone had wanted to know *exactly* what the message said, and she had been made to read it out, over and over again.

She looks down at her son.

Peace made it possible to have a family life and she can't wish the war back again. No, never.

'You are more special than anything, Sam,' she tells him.

'More special than Father Christmas?'

'Yes.'

'More special than the Queen?'

'To me and Dad, yes.'

'More special than God?'

'*Sam! You can't ask that!*'

'I'm hungry, Mum.'

'Heavens, is that the time?' Ellen looks at the clock. 'I must get your lunch.'

The water is making her hands sting. As she peels the potatoes, she thinks. *I had a moment of glory.*

I did.

For that second, Ellen longs to be back at Station 53 being congratulated by her friends.

Sam leans against her. His body is soft and warm and loving. Ellen looks down at him. Sam grins up at her and the gap in his teeth seems huge.

She smiles at him, dries her hands on her apron and bends down to give him a kiss. He smells hot and sweaty but lovely, and thoughts of the past fade away. What could be more important or exciting than her son?

This was what they fought the war for.

Birthday Secrets

Rowan Coleman

Michael David Henderson is my son. And he turns twenty-one today.

Michael David Henderson is also my husband. And he turns fifty today.

It seemed like such a good idea, all those years ago, when our only child was born on his father's twenty-ninth birthday.

'Let's name him after you,' I said.

'Brilliant,' he said, because I knew that he secretly loved the idea of living for ever through his children. And we knew then that Mikey would probably be our only child.

My two men, the two men I love more than anything, with the same name, the same birthday, but as different as chalk and cheese.

It was never a problem, my two boys having the same name, the same birthday and the same address. Not until Mikey turned eighteen, and a few weeks later we got a letter calling Michael D. Henderson to do jury service, but we had no idea which one. Even the court didn't know, just saying it would be OK if one of them turned up.

The two of them argued about it for days. Mikey was determined not to cancel his trip to Ibiza, and Michael went on about how important his job as a GP was. In the end Michael won, and it was Mikey who went to court, moaning that he was giving up his youth for the locals' sniffles and bunions.

Now we have two landmark birthdays on one day. A historic day for my little family.

A day of new beginnings.

I smile as I lie in bed next to Michael, who is still asleep with his back to me, snoring like he always does. He even snores as if he is terribly important, but that's always been his way. And he is a pillar of the community. People look up to him, though I think he's always found that it's a burden.

And Mikey. Well, it's taken Mikey a long time to step out of his dad's shadow and be confident about the kind of man he is. Now he's finally ready to stand on his own two feet.

Outside the sun is bright in a perfect blue sky, and everything feels just right. Yes, today is going to be a big day.

It's Mikey who picks up the cards from the doormat and brings them into the kitchen.

Michael watches his son as he begins to open them, ripping through the envelopes and tossing them onto the floor. I smile as I watch him. This is his last weekend living at home, and then he'll be gone for good.

He'll be moving into his own place with his mate, Joshua. Michael likes to slap him on the back and joke about what a good time he'll have in his own bachelor pad. Michael tries to be a friend to Mikey. If he stopped trying he'd do a much better job.

'Some of those might be for me,' Michael says, nodding at the cards that Mikey reads and then stands carefully on the table in a row.

'They're always for me,' Mikey grins. 'Mum and I are the only people who ever get you a card, and we're not going to post it, are we?'

'Yes, but today is my fiftieth and that's a big birthday,' his dad says, looking a little crushed. 'I might get at least one.'

'Fine,' Mikey splits the haul of birthday cards into two and slides a few across to his father.

'Birthday cake for breakfast!' I place the cake on the table. On one side, two candles make the number fifty, and on the other side, two more make twenty-one. Half is iced in Blue for City, and half in red for United.

'Really, Mum,' Mikey complains, 'I thought we'd get a cake each this year!'

'It's tradition, isn't it, Michael? Michael?'

But Michael isn't listening to me. He is reading one of the cards, except it doesn't look like a birthday card. It's plain silver with a purple question mark on the front. His face drains of colour, until it is almost grey.

'What's that?' Mikey tries to grab the card, but his father presses it against his chest, not wanting anyone to see it.

'Michael?' I reach out to him, putting my hand on his arm. 'The look on your face! You'd think it was an invitation to your own funeral!'

Slowly he lays the card flat on the table.

'Michael David Henderson,' it reads in neat capitals. 'Stop Keeping Secrets, they always come out in the end!'

'Well, how silly,' I laugh nervously, but neither man smiles. 'I don't get it. What's the punchline?' But there clearly isn't one. 'It must be someone's idea of a joke. Neither of you have anything to hide, do you?'

Silence.

'I mean you don't, do you?' I say again. 'Mikey?'

'Well,' Mikey says uncomfortably. 'There is *something* I've been meaning to tell you.'

'Is there, darling?' I ask. 'Go on then.'

'It's . . . about my final exams.' Mikey says. 'It's just . . . I don't know which one of my mates would want to do this to me, unless it was Rebecca getting her own back . . .'

'Rebecca?' I ask. 'That girl you were seeing?'

'Not any more. She took it quite badly.'

'Well, what about your finals?' Michael asked. He always likes to keep to the point.

'I . . .' Mikey sighs. 'Well, I didn't exactly pass them. I sort of mostly, totally failed.'

I gasp. 'But . . . that's not . . .'

Michael groans, but Mikey rushes on. 'But it's OK, it's fine, I've talked to Uni and I can take them again, which I'm going to do. And it hasn't made any difference to my new job. I've told them and they are fine with it, because they like me anyway. I just . . . I knew how much you were looking forward to wearing a hat to graduation, Mum. I'm sorry, I didn't want to let you down.'

'Oh, Mikey,' I said. 'I wasn't expecting that at all.'

'Well, that's thousands of pounds on your education down the drain!' Michael adds, with his usual lack of tact.

'You're one to talk!' Mikey shoves the card back at his father. 'When you read this you looked like you'd seen a ghost. What's *your* secret, dad?'

26

I turn my gaze to my husband. Twenty-eight years of being married to him means I know when he is hiding something, and he's doing that right now.

'Michael?'

'*I'm* not hiding anything,' he roars, sweeping the cake off the table in a gesture of anger that is not like him at all. It lands upside down, the plate cracking with a dull thump, cushioned by the soft plop of the ruined cake. Mikey and I watch as Michael thunders out of the room, slamming every door he can find.

'Tosser,' Mikey says.

'Mikey!'

'Mum, please can you call me Mike now that I am twenty-one?'

'This day isn't going at all like I thought it would,' I say.

He pauses, taking a breath.

'Mum, there's something else. Something I've wanted to tell you for as long as I can remember but I haven't known how ...'

Just at that moment Michael comes back in carrying a plastic bag. He tips it up on the table and out come several items of underwear. It's floaty and skimpy, reds, blacks, purples, fur trimmed and sequined, some of it barely there at all. I stare at the pile, and then at my husband.

'There,' he says. '*That's* my secret. Although I am amazed that you hadn't found out a long time before this. But now it's out, well, I don't care.'

My hands fly to my mouth.

'You're . . . having an affair?' I ask him through my fingers. 'With a tart!'

'No!' Michael sighs. 'No, I love you and only you. I thought last night would have proved that.'

'Oh God,' Mikey says. 'Please don't talk about your sex life in front of me.'

'Here. Now can you guess?' Michael puts a pair of red shiny high-heeled shoes on the table.

'You're having an affair with a giant?' Mikey suggests. And then his eyes widen. 'Oh my . . .'

'Sometimes,' Michael says. 'I like to dress as a woman.'

I stare at him.

'And call myself Francesca.'

No one says anything.

'And when I tell you that I'm playing squash on a Thursday night, I'm actually at a club for others like me. I can only think that one of the other people at the club sent this card to try and encourage me to be more honest about it. And although I never wanted you to find out this way, I'm glad that you have, because I've hated lying to you for all these years. It doesn't mean I don't love you, Sarah. It doesn't mean that I want another life, or someone else, another woman or a man. I don't. I love our life. It's just sometimes I like to love it in a skirt.'

Mikey laughs out loud, but not at his dad. He laughs with joy and something else, love and pride.

'Dad, that is awesome!' he says. 'This is so cool. Mum, don't you think that is cool? Dad isn't just some stuffed suit, he's actually cool!'

'So . . .' Michael takes my hand in his. 'I know this must come as a surprise . . . ?'

I pick up a pair of flimsy panties, which I can now see are an Extra Large. 'To be honest, I'm more amazed that you've not shrunk these in the wash,' I say.

'You're not going to leave me, are you?' my husband pleads. 'You don't hate me? Because I love you now just as much as I did on the day I first met you.'

'Well, if I haven't left you over your snoring, I'm hardly likely to leave you over some under- wear and some shoes,' I say, touching his face. 'You poor thing. I don't know why you didn't tell me sooner.'

'I'm sorry.' Michael says, looking sad.

29

'Can I come with you, to your club?' I ask him. 'Or is it just for, you know. Transvestites.'

'Would you come? I'd be so proud if you did,' Michael said. 'It would mean a lot to me.'

'I never knew my parents were so open-minded.' Mikey grins.

'Well, it's only clothes,' I say. 'It's what's inside that matters, Mikey, nothing else.'

'God, I love you guys,' Mikey says. 'I am so going to miss you when I move out.'

For a moment the two men that I love the most in all of the world stand either side of me and hug me tight. I feel the tears well up in my eyes.

'Which is why I have something else to tell you first,' Mikey says, seriously. 'Mum, Dad . . . Josh, he isn't my flatmate. He's my boyfriend.'

'*Finally*,' I say.

'Finally?' Mikey says.

'Well, I've been waiting for you to say something since you were about nine years old,' I say.

'It's true,' Michael says. 'We've talked about it a lot. We've been wondering when you'd feel able to talk about it.'

'You mean . . . You mean you knew I was gay? And you're fine with it?'

'Completely fine,' I smile. 'Although I still

want to have words with you about failing your finals.'

'So . . .' Mikey looks at the cake on the floor. 'Shall we go out for breakfast, my treat?'

'Sounds lovely,' I say, 'You two go ahead. I'll just clear up this mess.'

I wait for a moment, listening to the sound of my two men laughing in the hallway.

At last there are no more secrets. All of the things that were left unsaid for so long are out in the open, and that's the way it should be in a family. Well, except for two tiny little secrets that I will never reveal.

Firstly, I found my husband's stash of women's clothes ages ago. I knew his secret just as we have known our son's.

And it was me who sent that card.

Truth is Stranger than Fiction

Jenny Colgan

I'm a journalist on our local paper, and when people find out what I do, they always say 'Ooh! Truth is stranger than fiction.'

Then they tell me a very long and boring story about a parking ticket or something, which, I will tell you, is usually not at all strange. But here is the strangest story I did hear.

I was covering a diamond wedding anniversary, which is sixty years. My newspaper does lots of weddings and anniversaries, partly because they're nice, and partly because it means everyone at the parties buys a copy of the paper afterwards.

The elderly couple, in their eighties, were still living in their own home, surrounded by faded pictures and a spotless kitchen that was older than me. There was fizz, a nice card from the Queen, lots of relatives and excited children tearing up the place. The couple smiled at one another and held hands and I started to get a bit teary.

Because that is all there is in life in the end, really, isn't it? Sharing happy moments with your friends and relatives; walking arm in arm, the two of you, together till the end?

It wouldn't have hit me so hard if Joe and I hadn't been in the middle of divorce, the lawyers like crows, picking over the remains of our ruined lives.

The old man, whose name was Edgar, noticed me welling up, and patted me on the arm.

'You all right love?'

'Yes,' I said, pulling myself together and reaching for my notebook. 'Can I ask you a few questions, Mr Morris?'

'Of course,' he said. He glanced over at his wife, her neatly bobbed hair white as snow. She was sitting on the sofa with a very little child on her lap, who kept grasping for the thin gold locket round her neck.

'So, how did you two meet?' I said.

I remembered how Joe and I met. He was a policeman, and journalists have a lot to do with them. The night I saw him, he was helping out a young runaway who'd bowled up on the streets. It was freezing. Joe was asking him his shoe size, and ten minutes later he came back with a pair of stout boots from the Lost and Found box.

I fell for Joe right away. His gentle voice contrasted with his burly presence. My friends thought it was the most romantic thing they'd ever heard. I still had no idea how our marriage had collapsed in such a mess of stress and over-work and impatience.

'Ah,' said Edgar, shaking his head. His ears were huge and tufty with hair and he wore a hearing aid. 'Well, we met in the war.'

He glanced over at an old photograph on the wall. He was barely recognisable, Edgar as a young man, in full military uniform. He had a long row of medals on his chest.

'I was in the parachute regiment,' he said, casually. 'I was dropped into occupied France in 1943.'

'Wow,' I said. 'That's amazing. Right in the middle of the Second World War.'

Edgar smiled.

'You don't think of it like that when you're young. Felt like a big adventure back then.' He shook his head. 'Can hardly believe it myself now.'

'You were very brave,' I said.

'I was scared out of my wits,' he said.

He took a sip of a drink.

'It all went like clockwork, to begin with. There was a little pocket of the French resistance we knew should be waiting for us, and they were. They hid me in a barn cellar along with the apples. Their job was to get as much information about German movements to me as possible, and then I'd get lifted out. My French was good, and for the first week or so, it went according to plan.

'The farmer's name was Jean-Baptiste, and he wasn't much older than me. He had a friendly, suntanned face and a grin as broad as his shoulders. As the evenings wore on he would often wander down to the barn and we'd chat away. He was getting married, and he spoke of Cécile often. I didn't meet her, of course, as I couldn't go anywhere, but I knew he was happy about it.

'After two weeks, I had a clutch of useful information, and we had to get word out that I was ready to get picked up. It was Claude, the runner; it was him that went to deliver the news.

'And he didn't come back.

'That night was the longest I'd ever known. We sat, Jean-Baptiste and I, even though it was the night before his wedding day. We sat together, in the barn, voices low, just... waiting. Staring at the map. Wondering if Claude was going slow. Whether he'd twisted his ankle. Whether he'd been stopped by the enemy, the Nazis.

'By five in the morning the sun was coming up. It was a golden morning in France, like those paintings, you know? Sunflowers as far as you could see. Jean-Baptiste and I just stared at one another.

' "Better lie low today, friend," I said.

'He shook his head.

' "But it's my wedding day."

' "They might come," I warned. "They might come for all of us. If they have Claude. And if he's spoken up."

'Jean-Baptiste swallowed.

' "All the better reason not to be here,' he said.

'He stood up and we drank some real coffee he'd been saving, and the other farmhands came in with a brandy for Jean-Baptiste, and they toasted his health and his future.

'We were all toasting him when we heard the car pull up.

'They made a different noise, those German cars. You learned to recognise it fast. I ducked under my hiding place in the floor pretty damn sharpish.

'Only one soldier came in and walked around. I could see him through a chink in the floor. The other soldiers were up at the main house knocking on the door. The soldier I could see was just inspecting the barn. He counted everyone in.

Then he counted the number of empty brandy glasses littering the floor. And then he opened his mouth to shout.

'I still don't know who shot him. The noise was tremendous. We all ran for our lives, straight out across those fields of sunflowers, quick as we could. The shooting started up, but I couldn't think of it. Either they would get you or they wouldn't. I just ran and ran as if they were toy guns. To my right, I saw Jean-Baptiste. He looked sideways at me, his eyes desperate.

' *"Vive la resistance!"* he shouted.

' "Long live the resistance", I thought.

'And then there came a whistling noise, and Jean-Baptiste vanished, down amongst the sunflowers. But my body did not stop. Instead, I had a burst of speed, and made it to the alleyways in the ancient village and disappeared.

'When I glanced back, the soldiers had gathered around Jean-Baptiste's body, and my only thought was, get to the church; get to the church; warn his family; warn them all.

'I slipped in the side door of the old church.

'It was a beautiful church in St Melvyn. There were stunning old paintings on the walls and gold everywhere. It was dark and cool in the warm summer morning. The entire village was there, dressed in their best, or what was left of it after three years of occupation, and they gaped at me.

'The padré – the vicar – looked at me, confused and sweaty, as I did my best to gabble out the situation. Someone quickly shut the doors.

'Suddenly we all heard a whistle, and the sound of marching footsteps, and a banging on the doors.

'It was the padré's quick thinking that saved me. He pulled me into the vestry, tugged his own white shirt on over my bare chest; threw water on my face. Luckily I had little beard. Then he took from the side a garland of the white flowers which both men and women wore to get married in the region.

' "*J'arrive* – I'm coming!" he shouted grumpily as the German soldiers banged on the door again. The vicar moved out of the vestry, pushing me in front of him. I thought my heart would jump out of my chest. I thought he was turning me in.

'At the altar, Jean-Baptiste's fiancé – Cécile – was kneeling, her face hidden beneath the flowers on top of a heavy veil. Her face – what I could see of it – was very flushed. Silent tears ran down her cheeks.

' "Cécile," I said. "I'm—'

' "*Chut*!" said the padre crossly, forcing me to kneel in front of the altar. "Don't move!"

'He opened the church door, and I could hear him talking loudly to the soldiers.

' "What do you want? We are busy! This is a sacred event; a marriage!"

'I heard the soldiers enter, then hang around awkwardly at the back, clearly taken aback by the importance of the occasion.

' "We have been here all morning! We are prepared for the sacred sacrament of marriage, and you disturb us in a house of God!"

'The commandant muttered something which sounded like an apology. My heart was beating so hard I thought it would burst through my ears. I kept my head bowed, worrying about the red dust of the sunflower fields on my heels.

'The Nazi commander said they were looking for men who had escaped earlier. He sent several of the soldiers on to continue the search. But the rest didn't move. They stayed, watching, their eyes scanning the aisles and the doors.

' "Carry on, padre," the commandant said.

I watched the old man, lost in his memories.

'What did you do?' I asked.

'I didn't do anything,' he said. 'I stayed stock still, trembling with fright. And so the padré had to come back round the front . . . and carry on with the marriage service.'

'No way!'

'What could he do? They were standing right there.'

'He did the entire service?'

The old man repeated the words in French.

'Pour meilleur . . . pour le pire.'

'For better, for worse,' I guessed, although I had never been any good at French.

He nodded, tears clouding his eyes.

'And everyone . . .' he went on. 'Everyone had to pretend along with us. Pretend to be happy. And as we came out, the Nazis were watching the congregation of course, but for a runaway farmhand. Not a young bridegroom in a fresh white shirt.

'We had to march out straight past them, heads held high, smiles painted on, hearts beating like pistons. Cécile . . . Cécile was amazing. Inside, her heart was utterly broken.

'On the outside, she kissed me to hide my face, put her bouquet up in front of me and acted the happy bride. We went all the way out and into the car, and drove to her house, for Claude, now, was gone, and Jean-Baptiste was gone, and the Germans smashed the entire ring of the resistance in the area.

'Except for me. All those brave boys.'

Edgar rubbed his face crossly.

'But what about Cécile?' I said. 'What did...'

Edgar looked over, a small smile on his old lined face.

'Oh, it took a long time of course. A *long* time. Her family took me in and hid me. They had to. I think we were married two years before she let me kiss her.'

'And you've been married all this time.'

'Oh, nobody says marriage is easy,' he said, with a twinkle in his eye. 'People give up rather easily, don't you find?'

The sprightly slender woman with the white hair came over. Her accent was still strong after all these years.

'Ah, my Edgar,' she said, smiling. His face still lit up when he saw her. 'Are you boring our guest?'

'I wanted to talk about how we met,' he said. Her face changed.

'I do not like to talk of those things,' she said.

'But it went well,' I said.

'Oh yes,' she said. She touched the locket at her throat.

'May I see it?' I said. I am very nosy, like all journalists.

Surprised, she unclasped it and handed it over.

On the right-hand side was Edgar – young and handsome in the photo, normal-sized ears. On the left, an old and faded shot of a very young man with a suntanned face and clear, merry eyes.

'So I had two loves in my life,' she whispered.

I nodded.

'Thank you,' I said.

Then I snuck out into the garden and made a call.

'Joe,' I said. 'Joe. Don't hang up. Don't shout, please. Can we just talk?'

May Day

Philippa Gregory

I am so terrified that I cannot hear a word that he says. His fat moon face looks down on me kindly. His pursed strawberry mouth, wrinkled with age, repeats the words. Then out of a swirl of noise, as they bring in the May with carols, I hear him say: 'I am asking you to be my wife.'

It is not possible to refuse. This is the King of England. He was on the throne when I was born. I have never known the country without him. My sister has served as lady-in-waiting to five of his wives, has attended four of their funerals, has seen him age, grow fat, grow bitter, go mad.

I am keeping him waiting, and this is a man with no patience.

'I am still in mourning,' I stammer. 'I am a widow. I am so surprised.' His piggy eyes gleam. He likes surprises. He likes pranks and games, people in masks, people pretending not to know him and then crying out at his good looks, his grace.

'Who is this handsome stranger?' people say, as the fat old king limps into the room carrying the peeled white wands of the May Day, pulls off his enormous hat and unwraps a tent-like cape.

'I will speak to you again, next week. But it is good to woo a maid in Maytime.'

I am not a maid, I am a widow. And May Day has not always been a good time for this king to woo a wife. The May Day joust was when this springtime lover arrested his enchanting wife Anne Boleyn and sent her to her death.

'I am honoured,' I say.

I don't feel honoured, I think I am cursed. I go to the chapel to pray that I may be spared. I put my face in my hands and remember a time long ago, when I was a child in the royal schoolroom. We all had to study a saint, and our tutor called on me to tell the story of Saint Tryphine.

Saint Tryphine lived so long ago that nobody knows the truth of her story. They say she was married against her will to her father's enemy. Exploring her husband's castle, she found a locked door, and then another, and then another. Driven by female curiosity, she enters the first secret room, and before her is the skeleton of a woman, tatters of silk rags wrapped around her bones. In the next room is a woman lying on the floor, old bloodstains around her broken skull.

She opens the third door to find a woman tied to a chair; her thin body shows that she has starved to death. There are two more doors: one hides a woman drowned in a tub of old soapy water, her lips blue. Behind the last is a woman strung by her neck from a beam, her heels swinging forwards and back in the draught from the door.

Tryphine falls back from this horror. But she knows at once that these are his wives: her husband is a murderer. She cannot speak for fear. She dare not meet him at dinner.

She takes to her bed. She says that she is ill and cannot come down to the great stone hall with the blazing fire, the drunk men-at-arms, the maids getting out of their way. She hides under the covers in her fear. She cannot escape her husband's castle. There is nowhere she can go.

She dreams the dead wives come to her in sleep, their ghostly fingers pull at her sheets, their white lips whisper a warning. She gets up from her bed, throws a cloak around her shoulders, and goes out to the dark and unknown dangers of the forest.

'You are making this up,' says my tutor. 'You were asked to write the facts of the saint's life, not make-believe.'

'This is a romance,' I reply. 'The facts are only ever a part of a story. Wait till you hear what comes next!'

She is pregnant and near her time. She gives birth to her son. But her husband comes after her through the forest, tracking her like a wolf. Just as she always feared he would. Just as the ghostly wives warned that he would. And he kills them both.

'She doesn't save herself?' asks my tutor.

'No,' I say, a serious nine-year-old. 'She dies and so does her baby. But she is restored to life by God, and now she is a saint and so is her baby. They will live forever.'

'And what is her lesson for you?' My tutor nods at Princess Mary who is waiting for her turn to tell the story of her chosen saint. *'What does she teach us about a woman's duty?'*

I know that he means me to say that a woman must marry as her father commands. That a husband good or bad must be endured. That if you obey him, even if he kills you, you have done your duty as a woman and you will have your reward in the next life for your pain in this one. But I cannot say this. I am too proud and too young. 'Master Tutor, what I learn is this – no woman should marry a dangerous man.'

By the first week in May I have accepted the old king's proposal of marriage. I am to be his wife

– the sixth. And next May Day the court crowns me with blossom. I am Queen of England.

I bring together his three children, each of them from a different dead mother. I make a royal family: the Princess Mary, the little Princess Elizabeth, and the little boy Prince Edward, the only Tudor heir.

I try to be a good mother and a good wife; but sometimes I feel the ghosts of the other wives standing coldly behind my chair, watching when I dance.

He drowns me in treasure, bathes me in perfume, wraps me in violet velvet. I am to have anything that I want, books and teachers.

I am free to write, to study, to talk and even to dispute with him. He likes me to come to his rooms and discuss with the great men of the church.

He says that he loves my sharpness of thought, my sense of what is truly holy, my belief in the New Learning.

'Look at this.' My sister's hand trembles as she holds a single sheet of paper.

'What is it?' I am expecting a huge bill from the jeweller. But I can pay it; I have a queen's fortune. Nan is distressed for nothing.

'A warrant,' she says. 'A warrant for your arrest.'

I cannot breathe.

'The charge?'

'Heresy. They say you are reading and writing against the laws of God.'

The punishment for heresy is burning at the stake at Smithfield market where animals are butchered on a weekday and martyrs made on a Saturday. They burn people like me who study, people like me who believe.

I, who think like a scholar, did not think that I could be treated like them. I always assumed that nobody would ever come for me.

'Someone has dropped this in the corridor outside your rooms, to warn you.'

'The king will never allow them to charge me.'

In silence, my sister Nan shows me the king's signature and the date – May.

I feel my knees soften, the room swirls around me. I drop to the floor. 'Put me to bed,' I say quietly.

Like Saint Tryphine, I take to my bed and hide under the covers like a frightened girl. I remember my tutor asking: *but why did she go to bed?* And my answer: because, even if you're very naughty, they won't pull you out of bed to whip you. And he laughed. *Nobody would hurt you, Katherine Parr.*

The king hears I am ill and sends his doctor.

'Go to him,' Doctor Wendy whispers as my head falls back on the pillow. 'Tell him you are mistaken.'

'I am not.'

'Show him that you don't have a wrong thought in your head. No thought at all.'

The words slip into my feverish sleep. I dream that I am Saint Tryphine and the dead wives are all around me. There is the old one in her Spanish headdress, her face grooved with sorrow for the babies she has lost. After her comes the second wife wearing a necklace with a B and three pearl drops, around the little neck that was severed by the sharp French sword. The third wife pulls at the sheets of my bed. They were her sheets, this was her childbed and her deathbed.

The fourth wife still lives. She knew how to flatter the king into giving her freedom. But the fifth ghost is such a child she says nothing, her pretty mouth in a pout of fear. I see her ask for the execution block to be brought to her room so that she can practice putting her head on it, like a girl anxious to play her part.

All night the other wives weave around my bed, and in the morning I am ill with terror. If I were Saint Tryphine I would put on my cloak and run out to hide in the forest. But this is England, and I am at Hampton Court Palace.

The bells outside are ringing and everyone seems so vividly alive today, though it is the day that I am to be sentenced to death.

I dress carefully, my maids handing my scented leather gloves in silence as if I am to walk to the scaffold. My sister Nan goes with me to the king's room but leaves me at the doorway. The guards open the wide double doors, and I go in.

He is not alone. His friends are discussing religion and I know this is a trap. He greets me with a warm smile and invites me to explain my views on a passage from the Bible.

I sit and fold my hands modestly in my lap. I smile. There is no crowing cock, there is no Judas kiss, but there is a betrayal.

In the heat of the king's bedroom, among the stink of his rotting flesh and the sweet smell of his medicines, it is myself that I deny in a clear voice. I betray myself and my religion and my learning.

I tell the king that I know nothing, that I understand nothing, that a woman could never know more than a man. I tell him that a wife should always obey her husband. I say that I am a fool beside his wisdom, I come to his rooms only to learn. God sets a husband over a wife to be her teacher.

Every man, even the poorest, is closer to God than any woman. Men are in the image of God and women are their servants.

I humble myself completely. My mother's wisdom and courage I forget. I trade in all my learning and thought against my life. I say I know nothing – to avoid him asking what have I studied? What do I know? And what do I think?

I do all this so that I will not have to say I have studied my Bible. I know he is a tyrant. And I think that the people who obey him are cowards.

'And is it so, Kate?' the king – my husband – asks. He is delighted at my submission. I could have clasped my hands beneath his boot to show how low I have sunk.

'It is so.'

'Then kiss me, sweetheart,' he says.

That night the king takes me to his bed and I go, smiling. As he falls into a deep satisfied sleep the shadows walk across the ceiling. I dream of Saint Tryphine. I am in the forest with her but we are not afraid. We are walking through the trees and the dappled light falls on our path.

'Never marry a dangerous man,' she says to me quietly. 'And if you have to, then keep yourself safe. Say anything, do anything, keep yourself safe.

'And hope for a better world for our daughters.'

A Walk Outside

Matt Haig

It was all a bit silly.

Stuart never really understood it, or why it happened, but it did, every single time.

He would get to the front door and even before he turned the handle, his heart would start to go. He would look down at the shopping list and his hands would be trembling. The shopping list was always short. Milk, bread, tin of toms. But even though his memory was okay, he needed a list. It was almost like a security blanket.

He'd open the door. And then one of two things would happen. Either he would shut the door straight away and go back inside.

Or:

He would take a few steps along the pavement, then stop at the first lamp post, then he would close his eyes.

'I can't do it,' he would say. And he'd be right. Because seconds later he would be back inside the house.

He had been this way since Sarah died. Which meant he had been this way for a year, as today – 18 March – was the anniversary of her death. She hadn't even died outdoors; that was the weird thing. She had died on the sofa. Attached to tubes. She hadn't been outside once during her last five weeks, since she'd come back from the hospital.

And yet, from the day after the funeral until today he hadn't been as far as the first lamp post along the street. Alice, his daughter, had come to stay with him for a month but was now back in Australia. She might as well have gone to Mars, but she was happy, and there was always Skype.

Indeed, the great thing about modern technology was that you never needed to leave the house at all. Every week Stuart would order a shop from the supermarket. He had learnt to freeze some of the milk, so it would last the whole week, though sometimes he would forget to take it out of the freezer and have to wait till lunchtime before he could have his Shredded Wheat. He'd always imagine Sarah laughing at him, out of pity. And he'd think of her and have a soft smile or a hard cry, depending on the day.

But yes, the internet seemed to have been designed for people like Stuart, who feared and avoided going outside. Agoraphobics they were called. You didn't even need to have real friends any more. You could do all your socialising on Facebook. Not that he used Facebook that much. There were too many videos of cats. He liked cats, but felt if he was a cat he'd be a bit annoyed by it all. Still, the internet had managed to shrink the world to the size of a screen, and however sad that might be for other people, for an agoraphobic it was pretty useful.

Today though, was the day he was going to change. But he didn't realise it. Not at first.

It began like this. He was sitting in the living room. He had finished his bowl of Shredded Wheat. He washed up. He went to the window and looked out. There was a woman carrying some flowers. He felt guilt as he thought of the dead flowers beside Sarah's grave.

He stayed watching the woman for a while. He did this a lot, these days. Although he hated being outside, he was obsessed with the idea of it. He would stand a little bit back, and watch people. He realised how terrible this was. Being a man behind a window, watching a woman who didn't know she was being watched.

He supposed she was about his age. Mid-fifties. Maybe a bit younger. She was wearing a coat that was light enough to flap about in the breeze, and her hair was blowing around. She seemed a bit flustered. She stopped on the pavement to get something out of her wallet. He closed his eyes. He shouldn't watch her. He felt guilty as if he could feel Sarah watching him, so he looked the other way.

There was a man walking down the road. Well, possibly a boy. He was tall and walking fast. He was a healthy looking boy. Strong. Maybe he'd been signed up for a youth team but it hadn't gone right for him. Stuart always did this. Made up stories for people based on no evidence at all.

Anyway, he needed to order some shopping. So he turned away from the window to head upstairs to the computer.

Before he reached the first stair something happened.

There was a sound.

A woman, screaming.

Stuart froze for a moment. A very small moment, because already he was moving again, heading for the front door.

He opened the door. His heart was pounding before he was even doing anything. He hadn't been out of this door in 349 days.

And there he was, suddenly. Outside, walking. But soon he forgot he was outside and walking because he saw the woman – the same one he had just seen seconds ago – and now she was getting herself up from the pavement.

'Oh my God,' he said. Because what other words are there when you see someone has been mugged or attacked?

'He took my bloody wallet,' she said, pointing down the street. She looked so upset that Stuart couldn't bear it.

The woman wiped her face. 'He spat in my face.'

Stuart saw the young man disappear fast around the corner.

'I'll catch him,' Stuart said.

And then he started to run.

He sprinted past the first street lamp. Then the second. He was now heading towards the third. He was running fast, beyond the limits of where he could see from his window.

I'll catch him.

Why had he said that? What was he thinking? But he knew the woman was staring at him, and he was still caught enough in the moment to carry on, until the corner, anyway, and then the young man was nowhere to be seen. He stood there, looking around, feeling the terror of the outside world. He needed to get back inside. He needed to have a roof between him and the sky.

'I'm sorry!' he shouted back to the woman.

And he couldn't think of anything else to say so he said it again. 'I'm . . . I'm sorry.'

He walked over to her.

'Are you all right?'

'Just shaken,' she said. Her voice so fragile it could have come from the breeze. 'I'll be all right.'

'Were your cards in there?' he asked, as his heart raced faster than it had done from the running. The terror of all those houses and windows all around. All the potential danger – danger that had just been shown to very much exist – lurking all around. It was as if even the lampposts were invisible weapons in some secret war against him. But still, this woman had just been robbed and was shaken and he had to stop thinking of himself.

'Yes,' she said. 'My bank card. A debit card. But there's nothing on it hardly. And some cash. But not much . . . Ten. Maybe a bit more.'

'Right. Well, you should phone the bank when you get home.'

She nodded. Looked worried. And a bit sheepish. She was close enough for him to see the soft lines around her eyes. Around her lips too. Her hair was flecked with grey. He hadn't been this close to someone since Sarah . . . Well, apart from the supermarket delivery man. You don't really see people on the internet. Or Skype. Even when you see pictures of their faces you don't really see *them.*

'This sounds stupid,' she said.

'What does?'

'I just wondered if you could walk me home.'

He panicked. It was like being underwater. And there was dry land – his house – *right there.* The air felt so thin it was almost not there.

'I... um... I... You should go to the police.'

'No. I'm not up for that. I just need to go home.'

'I...'

'It's all right. I'm just being silly.'

He looked at her frightened face. 'No, of course,' he said. 'I'll walk you home. Where do you live?'

'May Street.'

It rang a bell. 'Off London Road?'

'Yeah.'

Stuart's mouth dried. He felt a bit dizzy. A bit floaty. As if he was a watercolour cut out onto a photograph.

And so they walked. Stuart's hands were clenched into fists, as if he was on a rollercoaster, which he kind of was. The woman's name was Rose. He got that much. But a lot of what she was saying was just noise. He could tell when he was meant to say a 'yes' or a 'no' or a 'that's terrible' but not much else.

At one point he began to lose control of his breathing.

'Are you all right?'

He leant against a wall. 'It's just asthma,' he lied.

'Have you got an inhaler?'

'No. No. But I'll be fine...'

They reached London Road, and it was crowded. People looked at them. They probably looked like a couple. Stuart felt terrified. But they made it all the way to Rose's house on May Street. It was a charmingly scruffy-looking house.

'It's a tip,' she said, 'or I'd invite you in. That's the trouble with living on your own. There's no one to impress.'

'Yes. I know about that.'

'Well, except the cat. And cats aren't too fussed about interior design.'

They stood there for a while, and there was a moment when the panic of being outside lifted.

'You really should tell the police, you know?'

'They've enough to deal with.'

'Well, it was a crime. It's their job.'

She looked at him and again seemed to want to say something else. But this time she didn't. She just said, 'Thank you.'

And without really thinking, he said 'Thank *you*.'

Rose seemed confused. 'What on earth are you thanking me for?'

'It doesn't matter,' he said.

Rose stared at him. 'Actually, if you could ignore the mess you are more than welcome to come inside.'

'I'd really better be going back,' he said.

'Right. Well, there's a craft fair on Saturday. At the church hall. Might not be your sort of thing, but I feel like I owe you at least a coffee.'

Stuart nodded and felt a kind of soft sadness. 'Sounds nice,' he said. 'I'll try and come.'

He started walking home and the anxiety was still there, and that sadness, maybe because the world contained boys who are out mugging instead of playing football. But there was also something else. A kind of faint triumph.

He was walking hurriedly, head down, when he realised that he had something to do. Something he should have done months ago.

And so he went to the florist on London Road and bought some lilies and ignored all the little invisible terrors of the world. He controlled his breathing and looked at the late afternoon sky, a thousand shades of red and pink, as he headed for the cemetery.

Love Me Tender

Veronica Henry

It would be funny, if it wasn't so sad.

He was booked to play at an anniversary party, when it should have been his own.

Twelve years today, they would have clocked up, him and Melanie.

When Dave first got the booking, he didn't want to do it. He wanted to stay in, nursing his wounds, drinking can after can of beer and then falling asleep hoping not to dream about it all.

Then he thought about the five hundred quid. He couldn't afford not to do it. He'd have to do a lot of haircuts to get that much money. Ten pounds a pop, he charged, so that was fifty haircuts. But this was one night's work.

So now, here he was, on a train, heading for Chester, where he was playing at a big party thrown by some very rich clients of his agent. The wife was an Elvis fan, and his gig was a surprise planned by her husband. They'd paid for his train ticket and were putting him up in the hotel for the night, which was nice.

The last time he'd been in a hotel was their holiday in Egypt, just before Melanie left him. He'd thought they were happy, as they sat by the pool sipping cocktails. Turns out they weren't. Or at least, she wasn't.

He wasn't going to think about her any more.

He got out his notebook and went through his set list one more time.

'Love Me Tender'. Ha! He'd tried that – being tender. Maybe if he hadn't been so nice? Was that where he'd gone wrong? He was soft. He knew he was.

'Hound Dog'. That was nothing, compared to what she ended up calling him. A loser. A waste of space. The worst mistake she'd ever made.

'I'm All Shook Up'. That was putting it mildly. The whole thing had turned him upside down and back to front. He didn't know which way was up any more. Everything he'd thought was real turned out not to have been.

'Suspicious Minds'. Yeah. Well. He should have been more suspicious. Instead of thinking that Bob was his best mate. More fool him.

Still. At least he still had Elvis. Elvis had never let him down. Dave was the best impersonator north of the Watford Gap, and he had never been busier. When he was Elvis, nothing mattered. When he was Elvis, the world was at his feet.

It was when he wasn't that life was hard. Like now, on the train, with his cheese and pickle sandwich, wondering what the point was and when things were going to change. When was he going to feel better? When was he going to stop thinking about Melanie?

A woman got on the train at Birmingham and sat in the seat opposite him. She was about thirty, with short hair and no make-up, wearing jeans and a fleece. She had a nice face, but Dave could imagine Melanie saying she didn't make the most of herself. Melanie thought all women should look their very best from the minute they got up. Dave sometimes wanted to tell her it was OK, he didn't mind seeing her without make-up and high heels, but Melanie wouldn't hear of it.

'I'm not going to let myself go,' she'd say.

He supposed he hadn't appreciated her efforts enough. No doubt Bob did.

The woman threw her case into the rack and sat down with a face like a wet weekend.

Blimey, thought Dave. We're a right pair.

She kept looking at her phone, scrolling through the texts, and sighing. Then she put the phone down on the table between them and a tear rolled down her cheek.

'You all right, love?' he asked.

'No,' she sighed. 'But you have to be, don't you? Life goes on.'

'I suppose so,' he said.

'Bastard,' she said, and he blinked, and she laughed and said 'Not you. My ex.'

'Yeah. Well. Exes. They're best off exes,' he said.

As she wiped away her tear, he saw 'GARY' tattooed on the inside of her wrist. She saw him looking, and rubbed at it.

'Seemed like a good idea at the time,' she said. 'I'd do anything to get rid of it now.'

She put her face in her hands and sighed. Dave reached out and touched her arm.

'You'll be all right, love,' he promised.

He knew it was wrong, to touch someone you didn't know on the train. But sometimes, when you were hurting, it was good to know someone else cared, even if you didn't know them. And instead of telling him to eff off, she looked up and smiled.

'He cheated on me. With my best mate.'

'Join the club,' said Dave.

'Why?' she asked. 'Why do they do it?'

'I don't know. But we're better off without them, I know that. Even if it still hurts.'

'Maybe.'

'We'll get through it.'

She shrugged, put in her headphones, and spent the rest of the journey looking out of the window. At Chester, she tugged down her case and ran off before he could wish her well.

He wasn't sure if he felt better knowing he wasn't the only one. Or if it made him lose any hope he had.

The hotel in the city centre was plush and expensive. Dave made the most of his room while he waited for his gig. He wasn't on till nine, after the dinner. He watched the giant telly, took a long bath, used all the stuff in the bathroom and ate all the nuts and chocolate in the minibar. He didn't drink, because he never had a drink until after he'd performed. He'd make up for it after, he thought.

At half eight, he went down to the room they had set aside for him to dress and wait. He put on his white suit with the silver trim, greased his hair, put on his make-up and his shoes. He checked himself out in the mirror and smiled.

'Looking good,' he told himself with a thumbs up, then put on his shades and picked up his guitar. He wasn't nervous. He never was. He was Elvis.

He played a blinder. The guests cheered and clapped. They didn't want him to stop. But he ran out of songs in the end. So he mixed with all the party goers, having his picture taken with the women and making them giggle, calling them darlin' in his fake Elvis accent. He loved it. He wanted to be Elvis forever.

For those few moments, he wasn't Dave the barber from Corby. He was a star. He was someone people wanted to be with. He was handsome and talented and desirable. He wasn't a loser, or a waste of space. Or someone whose wife had run off with his best friend.

At ten thirty, the host tapped on his glass and told everyone to be quiet for a special guest. The room hushed, the lights dimmed, and a spotlight came on the stage. Dave sat to one side and watched.

And from nowhere appeared Marilyn Monroe, blonde and radiant, in a tight red dress. She came up to the mike, and sang 'Happy Anniversary', in the style of Marilyn singing 'Happy Birthday' to the president all those years ago.

Wow, thought Dave. She was the real deal. She had Marilyn down to a T. She was a class act. Not some tacky fake who didn't quite pull it off.

There were plenty of those, but this girl shone like a star. Her blonde hair was like a halo and her lips were red. She was pure glamour.

And the crowd loved her. Like they'd loved him. They clapped and cheered. Only this time, it was the men who wanted their photos taken, their arms around her waist. She smiled and played the part, batting her lashes and pouting and blowing kisses.

'Let's get a picture of Elvis and Marilyn,' said the host, and Dave came and stood next to her. The two of them stood in the middle of the dance floor while their photo was taken and everyone cheered.

'You look amazing,' he told her.

'So do you,' she smiled back.

Someone brought them each a glass of bubbly, and when she put her hand out to take it, he saw the tattoo on her wrist. GARY.

'It's you!' he said.

'Who?' she frowned.

'You were on the train earlier. I was sat opposite you.'

She looked at him. 'Oh my God,' she said. 'I can't believe it.'

The two of them laughed.

'It's a funny old game, this, isn't it?' she asked.

'Sometimes it's easier not to be yourself,' said Dave.

'Tell me about it,' she said. 'My name's Annie.'

'Dave,' said Dave, and they shook hands.

'Turns out we've got a lot in common,' she said. 'Not just our exes.'

'Yeah.'

He looked around the room. The guests were dancing, talking, drinking. The lights had gone down again. No one seemed bothered about them any more.

'How about we sneak off?' he said. 'And go for a drink in the hotel bar?'

He looked at her. She looked nothing like the girl on the train. But then he looked nothing like himself, to be fair. It was amazing what a wig and make-up could do.

But she knew what he looked like in real life. She'd seen him on the train, without his costume and make-up and wig. This was the moment she would make a choice. He wasn't Elvis, the heart-throb. He was dull old Dave the barber.

He seemed to wait forever for her answer. He braced himself for a no, and thought he would go back to his room and drink the minibar dry. Then her face lit up. Her smile was wide and her eyes danced.

She took his arm, and he felt warm when she touched him.

'Let's go,' she said. 'I always thought Elvis and Marilyn would have made a great couple.'

The Promise

Andy McNab

I threw my overnight bag on the hotel's grubby bedcover and checked my watch. There was still time to kill but I didn't want to go out on the streets until I had to. They brought back too many bad memories. Instead, I collapsed on the rusty bed and rubbed my face in my hands. I wasn't sure if I was doing it to get rid of the tiredness or to wipe away the guilt.

I had left my private jet in its hangar so no one would know where I was heading. The sound of rat claws rattling across the wooden floor just outside my room reminded me I was a long way from home.

I checked my watch again. It was time to leave. With one last rub of my chin stubble and a quick swipe to get the sleep out of my eyes, I dragged myself off the bed and headed out.

I had made a promise to return to this city exactly twenty years ago today. I would never have turned my back on the first part of that promise given all that happened here. But I hadn't exactly stuck to the second part as well as I could have.

I remembered the back street shortcuts easily enough but it wasn't exactly a happy stroll down memory lane. Coffee shops and fashion stores had now replaced the bombed-out buildings. Families were out walking, talking and smiling. No longer running for their lives, or crouching low over their children to protect them from the gunfire. There were no decaying dead bodies lying in the streets either.

I turned a corner into an alleyway. Last time I walked over these cobblestones, they had been stained red with blood, and dogs were eating the remains of an old woman. It made me feel guilty and ashamed of my old life.

I stood outside our meeting place, a solid granite building. It was no longer a bank but a fancy pizza parlour. I could still see the bullet strike marks and artillery shrapnel scars chipped into the stone. I was on time. Well, five minutes early, which counted as military 'on time' anyway.

Jez turned the corner, I checked my watch. It was 15.58 – or two minutes to 4.00 p.m. as I had switched to calling it for the last twenty years.

'Mate, you're getting slack.' I tapped the face of my watch with a forefinger.

'Three minutes late.'

Jez gave a smile from a face that life had been chewing on since we last met. We shook hands. It felt good to see him.

Jez was as curious about me as I was about him. 'I call myself John now. It's close enough to Jez, so I can remember. What's your new name?'

'William.'

Jez looked me up and down for a second. 'Nah, don't like it, doesn't suit you. You'll always be a Tony to me. Let's stick to real names today, eh?'

We checked out the passers-by and Jez looked concerned. 'Where's Mick?'

A church bell struck in the distance as a young man, maybe seventeen or eighteen years old, approached us. He looked clean cut, with short brown hair, maybe a dozen zits on his face. He was holding a blue sports bag.

'Are you Tony and Jez?'

We nodded, letting the boy do the talking as he unzipped the bag.

'I'm Tom. Dad told me that even if he was dead, he had to be here. I have no idea what this is all about but here he is.'

He opened the bag to reveal a stainless steel urn, presumably with Mick's remains in it. Then he pulled two white envelopes with our names on, out from under the urn. 'Dad wanted me to give you these. He said both letters are identical but just in case one of you didn't make it...'

I pulled out the single sheet of paper in mine, and started to read as the automatic doors to the old bank ushered us in.

Mick's letter said he needed my and Jez's help. He wanted us to tell Tom all about his past, so he could wipe the slate clean. He said that Tom was a good lad and tougher than he looked, so we shouldn't hold back. Oh, and by the way it wasn't Mick anymore. It was Simon.

We all sat down at a table for four and Tom placed his dad on the table in front of the empty seat.

He shrugged his shoulders. 'It's what Dad told me to do.'

I thought it was funny. 'Yeah, he wants a front row seat now he doesn't have to pay for the pizzas.'

The bad joke got a laugh at least, and we ordered our food and beer before I leant over to Tom.

'Did your dad tell you who we are and why we are here?'

Tom shook his head. 'What's this all about?'

I pointed to the urn.

'Twenty years ago your dad used to go by his real name, Mick.'

Jez, who had also read his letter by now, joined in our double act.

'Your dad wanted you to know about his past. We are going to give it to you straight. It's always the best way. Me and Tony gave ourselves new names for our new lives too, just like your dad.'

I didn't wait for a reaction from Tom. I explained that the three of us had joined the army together when we were sixteen, and we all left after five years when we found out we could earn more money fighting as mercenaries.

'Your dad became the leader of a team of nine of us. There were some Germans, Russians and a French guy. We started off fighting for the government's forces, supporting the people who lived in this city. But then we were offered more money to fight for the other side, so we switched sides without a second thought. We carried out attacks on the city night after night for almost a year, causing so many deaths. Then one night, purely by chance, we caught and questioned a government soldier, and we learnt that over $30 million was being held in a bank, the very building we are sitting in now. From that moment on, our team of nine had a new plan because we thought that stealing money would be simpler than fighting for it.

Jez took a swig of beer before taking over the story.

'We were wrong. We put our plan into practice. Stole the money easily enough but our getaway turned messy. Six of our team were killed by security guards in a huge gun fight as we tried to exit the bank with backpacks stuffed with the cash.'

Jez waved his hand out over the room towards a group of happy, smiley people, stuffing their faces with pizza.

'The worst of the shooting took place here, right where we are now. Your dad, Tony and I managed to fight our way out and we escaped with the cash back to the UK. But we never felt right about it. All those guards dead, plus our six mates, plus all those people we had killed during the war. We couldn't enjoy the cash even though we tried. Every time we went to buy some flash car or expensive holiday, we couldn't go through with it.'

Jez slumped back into his chair and I could tell he was feeling that same guilt all over again.

I waited for Tom to turn and face me so I could continue.

'To make ourselves feel better and atone for the guilt, Mick decided we would split what was left of the cash evenly between the three of us.

He then made us promise that we would do our best to become good people and use the money wisely to help others in the future. This promise, we all agreed, would be like a payback for all the lives we had taken during the war. It also would somehow honour our dead mates.'

I also explained that his dad had made us promise that we would all meet up in exactly twenty years time, at the exact hour that we had originally attacked the bank, and account for what we had done with our lives and the money.

'So what did your dad do with his money, Tom?'

Tom's cheeks coloured as he spoke. He was taking the news well, just like his dad thought he would.

'My dad was a good man. A great dad too. He spent every single day helping others. He worked non-stop for charities that build homes for the homeless and the elderly. He was always giving cash to parents of children with cancer too, so they could go to the best hospitals for treatment wherever that was in the world. Mum and me could never work out how he ever found the cash. We weren't poor but we weren't exactly rich...'

Tom's voice trailed off. He changed tack,

picked up his knife and fork and began to dig in to his pizza.

I asked him a tough one. 'Do you forgive your dad?'

He put the cutlery down again as he sat and thought for a while.

'My dad may not have started his life off well but he kept his promise. He did the right thing. And he did the right thing for the best part of his life. How can I be angry with him for that?'

Jez had barely touched his pizza either. He leant in and spoke in a hushed tone.

'I tried to do the right thing with the best part of my life but it just never worked out that way. What I thought was kindness got taken as weakness. Somehow, I always seem to get ripped off. Nearly all the money I had, I ended up spending on bad business deals and expensive divorces. I've let everyone down. I really tried but...'

He looked down as he picked up his glass and gulped at his beer. We all sat and stared at our plates for a bit. It was Tom who broke the silence. 'What about you Tony?'

I didn't answer for a while. I was thinking.

Jez joined in too. 'Tony, mate. What about you?'

I took a breath and prepared to make the biggest decision in my life so far.

'Things went well for me. I have a family that I love. And I am about to sell my various businesses and if all goes well, I'm going to end up with more money than I'll ever need. But the thing is, everything I have ever done has been for my family. I haven't helped people like Mick. I haven't even tried to like you have, Jez. So, I haven't really been as true to the promise as Mick but maybe I still can be ... I need to make this right.'

I took a mouthful of beer and fixed my eyes on Jez.

'Let's take one more shot at this. I will come clean to my family about who I am, and hope they forgive my past, just like Tom has. Then why don't all three of us carry on Mick's great work. We'll use my money to fund the work. But I need your help, Jez. And yours too, Tom, if you're up for it?'

Tom nodded eagerly. He flushed with pride at the thought of continuing in his dad's footsteps. Jez too broke into a smile. 'Count me in. I'm going to do this right this time around, and we've still got time to make it good.'

All three of us raised our glasses, and with it, the burden was lifted.

'To – The Promise.'

The Crater

Richard Madeley

She'd passed it dozens, no, hundreds, of times on the way to the bus stop to catch the double-decker that took her to work. But she'd never really seen it – not until she fell asleep on the top floor of her bus back home. It had been a long day teaching her class of nine-year-olds and she had stupidly missed her stop.

She'd woken with a start to see a gap in the curving Victorian terrace of houses that some-how she'd never noticed before. From up here, it looked like a missing tooth in a wide smile. There must have been a house there once, surely? Why would those long-dead builders have left a gap like that?

As she stood up, she thought she glimpsed a shadowy circle on the grass that grew in the empty space. But then her bus turned a corner, and the view was lost.

That was on Friday, so it wasn't until Monday that she found herself walking past the gap in the terrace. From ground level there was no sign of the strange circle she thought she'd seen in the tangled grass between the two houses. She would have stepped into the space – there was no fence or hedge – to have a closer look, but that would have meant missing her bus. The headmistress took a dim view of teachers who arrived late for the staff meeting before assembly. The last time it had happened the old bag's icy disapproval had been well below freezing.

'I don't accept excuses for lateness from my pupils and I certainly won't accept them from my staff, Susan,' she'd said, in front of the entire staffroom. 'If you are late again this term you will have to take the consequences. Which I assure you, you will not like.'

Witch. Bitch. Cow.

So it was not until that evening that Susan felt free to pause on her walk home from the bus stop and stare at the mysterious gap between the houses. Although the sun was setting it was still light, and after only a moment's hesitation she stepped off the pavement and onto the knotted grass and weeds.

She realised, straight away, there HAD been a house here, once. She could feel what was left of it, blindly pushing up under the earth and rank weeds, like a child's toys hiding under a blanket.

Beneath her feet, clad only in their light summer shoes, she felt . . . what? Bricks? Bits of wood? And – yes, over there, poking out under a tall thistle, she could see a broken roof-tile.

Had there been a fire? A gas explosion? What could have destroyed, with such finality, the home that once stood here? And why were the houses on either side unscathed?

Clouds were blowing up out of the west and the sky was darkening. She took her phone from her handbag and switched it on, using its light to cast around, searching for the strange circle she thought she'd spotted from the top of the bus three days earlier.

But she could see nothing, apart from patches of nettles and the odd crisp packet that had blown in from the road. For some reason she was certain no one ever came here. Susan wasn't a superstitious person, but she had learned to trust her instincts. There was something . . . well, wrong, about this spot. Not frightening – not in the least – but wrong. Sad, and somehow more than that. Empty. Sucked away. Lifeless.

She shivered.

Time to go home.

'What do you mean, "altitude survey"? What are you talking about, James?'

She'd phoned her brother, who only that month had qualified as a surveyor.

He laughed. 'It means, my little crosspatch, that you can learn a lot more about a site from the air than you can on the ground.'

'Really?'

She couldn't see him, but she knew her brother was giving his trademark double-nod of agreement.

'Yes, they can. Only last year a bunch of historians researching the site of a Saxon village came to a dead end. So they hired a microlite and a pilot to do a few circuits overhead and took pictures. The results were astonishing. They could see the outlines of roundhouses, grain stores, animal enclosures. Tons of stuff you couldn't make out at ground level.'

Susan smiled. 'So you think I should get a hang-glider and float around above Windsor Terrace taking happy snaps?'

James laughed.

'No – but I DO think you should take your camera back onto the top deck of the number forty nine and grab some pictures as you trundle past. Download them to your laptop and send them to me. I'm not promising anything, Susie, but I might be able to tell you what that circle of yours means. Or, rather, a friend of mine can.'

It was no good. The bus was much too bumpy to get anything close to a clear shot. Susan didn't even consider sending the blurred photos to her brother.

It was while she was walking back home, past the empty square of grass, that the idea struck her. The people living in the terraced house on the left side of the space had built a loft extension with a big glass window that looked down on the vacant lot. It was even higher than the top floor of the bus. If the owners would just let her go up there . . .

Two minutes later she was knocking on the front door of 14, Windsor Terrace. A middle-aged woman with a worried expression opened it.

'Yes?'

Susan took a deep breath.

'Hello. I live in Cranfield Gardens round the corner . . . I teach at St Cuthbert's. My name's Susan Fisher.'

'Yes?'

'Well . . .' She paused. This was going to sound silly.

'Well . . .' she said again. 'The thing is . . . I was going past here on the bus the other day and I saw – from the top deck – into the . . . that garden-sort-of-thing next door.'

84

She swallowed, and pressed on.

'Anyway, I hadn't noticed it before but from up there' – she waved vaguely into the air behind her – 'I thought I could see a sort of circle in the grass. It's been fascinating me ever since and I'd like to photograph it. I was wondering if you'd let me do that from your dormer window up there. It should give a perfect view down.'

To her surprise the woman relaxed and smiled agreement.

'Oh yes, please do! My husband and I had that window put in last summer and the first thing we noticed when we looked out was that circle. We think it looks like the marks of a giant campfire. Our daughter says it's an evil fairy ring! But really we have no idea what it is. Do you?'

Susan shook her head.

'No, not at the moment. But I may be able to find out.'

It was only when she was leaving with her phone full of photos that she realised the house on the far side of the empty space was marked as number 18.

So there had been a house here once.

Number 16.

'It's all perfectly simple, sis. No mystery at all, I'm afraid.'

Down the line Susan heard her brother cough with false modesty. She loved James but, God, he enjoyed playing the know-all.

'Well go on, tell me then.'

'Certainly . . . well . . .' He drew the moment out as long as he could.

'Well,' he repeated, just as she was about to explode with impatience. 'Turns out it's a bomb site. You know, from the last war. I emailed your photos to a mate of mine who's really into World War II stuff. Sent him the address, too – 16, Windsor Road, Clapham. He did a bit of research online and came up with the goods. It's all in the official war records and even the local papers from back in the day.'

'What happened?'

'German parachute mine, dropped one night in November 1941. Wasn't even during a big raid. Nasty, low-level sneak attack, so the air raid sirens hadn't sounded. Bomb floated straight down on top of number 16, crashed through the roof and both floors and exploded slap bang in the middle of the house. Killed everyone inside outright. That ring you can still see is what's left of the blast crater.'

She swallowed. 'That's awful. But why weren't the other houses knocked down too?'

'Dunno. Turns out bomb-blast is a funny

thing. Quite often buildings near an explosion like that get away with broken windows and a few missing tiles.'

Susan thought for a moment. 'You said there were casualties?'

'Sadly, yes. A young family, the Greenfords. Tom and Elsa, and their twin baby boys, Peter and Harold, three days old, too young to be evacuated from London. Father was home on special RAF leave. There may have been an older child, possibly a daughter, but the records are vague about that.'

'And this happened when, exactly?'

'Just a minute.' She heard her brother tapping on the keys of his laptop.

'Yes,' he said after a few moments. 'Like I said, November 1941 ... November the ... well, I'll be damned! The 23rd! That's tomorrow night, Susie! How extraordinary! Maybe you should go and pay your respects, eh? Perhaps all this was, you know, sort of meant.'

She nodded, but didn't reply.

She knew exactly what she had to do.

It was a poor time of year for flowers but she found some nice roses at the florist in Church Street and borrowed a powerful torch from the school caretaker. James had told her that the

German bomb had gone off just before midnight, and a few minutes before the hour Susan was stumbling across the broken ground towards the dead centre of the crater.

When she got there she suddenly felt foolish. Why was she doing this? It was more than seventy years since the Greenfords had been blown to atoms. There must have been a funeral of sorts, perhaps a public memorial service. What possible good could she do now with her torch and silly flowers?

She bowed her head and tried to say a prayer. But no words came, and after a few moments she simply whispered: 'I'm so, so sorry', and turned to leave.

She caught her breath. A glowing light was moving towards her from the direction of the road. It was pale and indistinct, and seemed to hover above the ground.

Susan did not believe in ghosts, but suddenly she wished she could be anywhere but here.

Now she could hear a faint, rasping voice. The voice of a woman; a very old woman. It drifted across the broken ground towards her.

'Who's there?'

Susan felt her scalp prickle. Icy tingles flowed down the backs of both hands.

She struggled to speak and when her voice came, it was oddly thick and slow.

'My name's Susan . . . Susan Fisher. I'm a teacher. I'm . . . I'm only laying some flowers here, that's all. I'm doing no harm to anyone, I promise.'

The flickering light swayed closer. Susan could now hear a wheezing coming from behind it. She thought she might faint, especially when the croaking voice spoke again, more harshly.

'Why? WHY are you here? This is MY place, on this, this of all nights . . .'

Summoning all her courage, Susan pointed her torch at the approaching light. She gasped at what she saw.

It was an ancient, hobbling woman. She carried a battered hurricane lamp in one hand and a small and faded bouquet of flowers in the other.

The old woman's voice was now much clearer. 'I don't understand. You're frightening me . . . Why are you laying flowers? I've never seen you here before, or anyone else for that matter. What are you doing here?'

Susan felt her fear begin to ebb. 'I told you . . . I only recently found out what . . . what happened here . . . during the war . . . the tragedy. I wanted to pay my respects. Who are you?'

The old woman moved closer, silently staring into the eyes of the young teacher.

Finally, she spoke.

'I'm Elsa Greenford.'

My God, she *is* a ghost, thought Susan, her hands and scalp beginning to prickle again.

'A husband and wife died here, seventy-three years ago tonight,' the hunched figure continued. 'So did their babies. They were my family . . . my parents and my brothers. But I wasn't with them. I'd been sent to the countryside, you see.'

Susan exhaled and slowly nodded. 'Yes, yes, I see . . . you're the surviving Greenford, aren't you? The missing daughter . . . you weren't here that night . . . but surely – surely it was Elsa who died?

The woman opposite smiled. 'I was christened Elizabeth, but after my mother passed I took her name. It's all I had left of her.'

Susan impulsively dropped her torch and reached forward with both hands, repeating the words she'd spoken, alone, a few minutes earlier.

'I'm so, so sorry.'

'Yes . . . well . . . I lived . . . and they died. All four of them. In an instant. I'd never even seen my baby brothers . . . they were born after father and mother sent me away.'

She lifted her head, almost proudly.

'I've been coming here each November almost ever since. Alone. Always alone. Until tonight.'

She paused, before suddenly giving Susan a small, shy smile. 'Until tonight,' she repeated. 'Thank you. Thank you for remembering them, too.'

And together, hand in hand, the two women gently placed their flowers to the ground.

The Gospel According to Judas

John O'Farrell

It would seem that I did not get my own gospel in the Holy Bible. I'm not bitter. Not bitter at all. Oh yes, Matthew, Mark, Luke and John all got their stories accepted. Paul wasn't even there and gets whole sections to himself.

But when I offered to tell my version of the story, the Bible editors were like, 'Oh thanks Judas, um, that's a really kind offer, but the thing is we've already got plenty of versions of that whole "Life and Death of Jesus" thing, so I don't think there's room for another one.' Bastards!

But *I was there*. I lived through the whole thing. My voice deserved to be heard too. Clearly they were too worried about how that might look, that it might taint the whole 'Holy Bible' brand to have one 'Gospel According to Judas'. Honestly, you betray just *one* Son of God...

Actually we *all* betrayed the Son of God, that is the point, but sadly no one seems to have got the deeper message within the writing. They were still seeking out simple Good and Evil instead of seeing that both forces are at play within all of us all the time. *Uncertainty* – that's what makes a good book. But people read the Bible and call it '*The* Good Book', capital letters, and see no uncertainty in it at all.

So I can't help being a little bit cynical when I look back at it all ten years later. Yes, it was amazing to be one of his twelve followers in those heady days of Our Lord. I was as devoted to him as anyone. We really thought we were going to change the world! But we were young back then. We had all these ideals. That sort of zeal is always going to fade over time.

We had a tenth anniversary reunion last month. All the Disciples got together for dinner exactly one decade on from the famous Last Supper.

I have to say we'd all done pretty well for ourselves, one way or another. Of course ten years earlier, we would have been outraged if we had thought any of us would ever get jobs working for the Romans. But we are all a bit older now and everyone has to make a living. Things just didn't seem so black and white as they had done when J.C. was around. I mean we would never have paid for a couple of strippers at the original Last Supper. 'You-Know-Who' would have got all moral about it. But ask any of us which was the better knees-up, and frankly I think we would all agree it was the one with the girls and drinking games.

In truth, the original Last Supper was more like a dull dinner party. I seem to remember we spent most of the evening talking about house prices. Andrew moaned that no one else had thought to bring a salad. James wanted us to reuse the starter plates for the main course to save on washing up. And not one of the written accounts of the Last Supper include the hour we spent listening to Peter telling really dull fishing stories. For ages we all thought there must be some deeper religious meaning to it all, but there wasn't; he really was just going on and on about fish.

But, of course, none of that made it into the Gospels. At least, not the final draft anyway. So all I'm saying is, real life doesn't happen like it does in the Bible. In real life, water does not turn into wine, water just turns into smelly water. The Jesus I knew wasn't perfect. He was actually a little bit, well, *preachy* if truth be known. And Pilate? Well he isn't so bad when you get to know him. He's got a very difficult job, and if he didn't wash his hands of a few things he'd never get anything done.

And sure, the death of Our Lord was a tragic and brutal event and we were all very upset about it at the time. But we all knew what the Romans were like. They were a bunch of fascist bully boys. When a few drunken soldiers were staggering down the road at night, you stepped into the gutter to get out of their way. If stopped and questioned, you gave short, polite answers. You did not come over all superior and say to a bunch of armed Roman thugs, 'I forgive you, for I am the son of God, and king of the Jews.' That was bound to really annoy them.

But anyway, that was it. Jesus Christ had been executed. It was over. I could see that we'd all be going our own ways. And then Matthew announced that he was going to write the one true version of the life of Our Lord. Just like that! No discussion.

Mark wasn't happy about this at all. He said he'd already been taking notes all the way through. Luke was always a bit jealous of those two, so now he tried to claim that Jesus had spoken to him in a dream ordering him to write the story of his life. And then John pipes up, 'Actually I've already got a publishing deal, so I'm the one writing the greatest story ever told'.

'Well we can't all write it. You can't have four versions of the same story all in the same book.

What if they don't line up?! What if there are differences!? That's going to cause all sorts of arguments...'

But they did all write it. And the sad thing was they were all really rubbish writers. You should have seen their first drafts; not one of them could string a story together, they were dull and repetitive, and of course none of them missed a chance to settle old scores or big up their part in it all.

Now you are probably thinking 'Oh here's Judas with the kiss-and-tell gospel, about to claim he did nothing wrong, it was all everyone else's fault.' But no, I accept my share of the blame for what happened. But I would also like to take some of the credit for what happened after. Because it was me who took those rubbish first drafts of the gospels according to Matthew, Mark, Luke and John. And I completely rewrote all four of them.

I didn't waste those thirty pieces of silver. I spent them on creative writing classes. I'd always seen the adverts; 'So you want to be a writer?' I thought I'd give it a go. The three-day course promised to teach me all about story structure, characters and voice. It made me ask myself some very basic questions:

'Who is the hero of your story?' Well, that was an easy one. Jesus.

'What does your hero want?' Hmmm ... only to save all of mankind for ever.

'What is your hero's flaw?' I don't know; a bit *holier than thou* maybe?

I completely reshaped the gospels so they followed the basic rules of good story structure.

'How is your hero an orphan in Act One?' Well, his real dad isn't around; he's in heaven.

'During Act Two, how does your character go from being a wanderer to a warrior?' Hmmm ... there *is* a lot of wandering, but it's sort of in the wrong place.

'And how is your character a martyr in Act Three?' You'd think that was easy, wouldn't you? He gets crucified, it's all laid out for you. But it only looks easy now – in the first drafts the crucifixion felt really random. My tutor kept saying to me 'Yes, but what is the *meaning* of these events – how do they advance your story, impact upon the other characters, what do they say about your theme?'

During the afternoon session called 'Creating Great Scenes', I wrote down 'Healing the Blind Man', 'Washing the Feet of the Beggar' and of course, 'The Feeding of the Fifty'.

'Go bigger!' the tutor said. 'More dramatic!'

'The Feeding of the ... 500?'

'Five thousand! Come on, your hero is supposed to be the Son of God, not some mid-size catering outfit.'

I said I was worried about keeping the whole thing credible.

'Ah ...' she said, 'You would be amazed what people will believe.'

And when my rewrite of their four gospels was completed, Matthew, Mark, Luke and John couldn't believe how much I had improved their versions; they were like 'This is a miracle!' which I thought was a bit lacking in respect given the subject matter. And then they read on and said 'You've made yourself look really bad ...'

I said 'Yes, because it's important to the story.'

'And you've taken out all of Peter's stuff about sorts of fish.'

'Yes, because it wasn't important to the story.'

You see, I learnt that there are rules. There are writing tricks and devices and if you master these, your story can have the power to move people to tears, to provoke anger, sorrow, laughter, to make people really believe. To make them ready to die for a cause that they weren't even aware of the day before.

The funny thing is that before they saw my rewrite, most of the other disciples were going off the whole Christianity thing – they were feeling a bit bored by it all. It was reading my final draft that got them all fired up again – made them ready to revive the religion and spread the word.

Then people who came across the stories from the Bible for the first time were captivated. They were convinced of their truth and ready to fight anyone who questioned a single word. My tutor told me that's what really good storytelling does. It makes people sure that it must be true.

I said 'Well, some of it sort of happened, some of it I've exaggerated and quite a lot of it I've just made up to point out a greater truth. So . . .' I asked her, 'does that make the Holy Bible fiction or non-fiction?'

'Like I taught you,' she said, 'always *uncertainty*'.

I don't mind that others get credit for what I did. I agreed a small fee based on sales, and the Bible is quickly becoming the best-selling book of all time. So I've already earned a lot more than thirty pieces of silver, I can tell you. And I allow myself a little smile whenever someone refers to 'Matthew Chapter 28, Verse 20' or 'John 3:16' as I hear my words not theirs.

John's original 3:16 went like this: *'And then, wouldn't you know it, one of the other blokes being crucified, the one on the left I think it was, well he wouldn't stop wailing and we were like, "I know it must be painful and you're dying and all that, but it's really not all about you today, all right?" And then this bloke's family objected to us saying he should be quiet and there was some pushing and shoving and then of course, it all kicked off...'* I like to think my shorter line about how God 'so loved the world' is a little more dignified.

It no longer bothers me that the Bible doesn't include The Gospel According to Judas. Because I know, and the other guys know, that all four gospels retell the whole thing according to the one bloke who learnt how to write.

That's when the stories started to have some real impact across the whole Roman Empire. *Saint* Peter, by now a big celebrity and head of a whole new religion, started to get a little bit worried. He said to me at our anniversary supper, 'What if people find out that you rewrote it all, that none of it happened quite like this; that some of it never happened at all?' I said 'Peter, *this is me*, Judas. I'm not going to betray your trust.'

Oh, well – not until now anyway.

Anniversary Recipes from The Hairy Bikers

We hope that you enjoy our menu: the cheese straws a tasty tempting nibble, the starter healthy, the mains and pud just downright lovely. The secret to cooking a meal is preparation. Do all your shopping from your list, and prepare all your ingredients and have them to hand. Then simply follow the recipe and you will have a meal to be proud of.

With good wishes from Si and Dave

Jumbo Cheese Straws with Gorgonzola, Parma Ham and Celery Seeds

These are great served with soup or as nibbles with pre-dinner drinks. Easy to make, but we warn you – make plenty.

Makes about 18
1 x 375g pack of puff pastry, defrosted
3 slices of Parma ham
100g Gorgonzola cheese
1 free-range egg, beaten
1 tbsp celery seeds

Roll out the puff pastry into a thin sheet. Cut the Parma ham into strips – keep them thin so that when you bite into the straws you don't pull out a big stringy bit of ham as you tuck in. Preheat the oven to 200°C/Fan 180°C/Gas 6.

On one half of the pastry lay out the ham, then crumble the Gorgonzola over the ham. Fold the rest of the pastry over the filling, like a sandwich, and roll out thinly again. Trim the edges square. Brush with the beaten egg and sprinkle with celery seeds. Cut into strips about 1cm wide. Take each strip and twist it into a spiral, then lay it onto a baking tray. Press down the ends slightly to make sure the cheese straws don't uncurl. Bake for about 20 minutes until golden. Leave to cool slightly if you can manage to hold people back!

Mushroom, Feta and Tomato Baked Peppers

It's always important for food to look good, whether you're dieting or not, and these peppers are a delight to the eye as well as the tastebuds. A great vegetarian recipe, this has lots of strong flavours that come together in a beautifully colourful and well-balanced dish.

Serves 2
4 sun-dried tomato pieces in oil, drained well
2 tsp sunflower oil
175g chestnut mushrooms, wiped and diced
20g blanched hazelnuts, roughly chopped
1 garlic clove, peeled and crushed
50g dry white breadcrumbs
½ small bunch of parsley, leaves finely
   chopped
1tsp dried chilli flakes
100g feta or soft goat's cheese, drained
2 smallish peppers, red or yellow
Freshly ground black pepper

Preheat the oven to 220°C/Fan 200°C/Gas 7. Roughly chop the sun-dried tomatoes. Heat the oil in a large frying pan and stir-fry the mushrooms over a high heat for 4 minutes.

Add the roughly chopped hazelnuts and fry for a further minute until the nuts are lightly toasted. Season with a good grind of black pepper and remove from the heat.

Stir in the tomatoes, garlic, breadcrumbs, parsley and chilli flakes until thoroughly combined. Break the cheese into small chunks and toss them through the stuffing lightly. Cut the peppers in half from top to bottom and carefully remove the seeds and membrane.

Place the peppers in a small foil-lined roasting tin, cut side up, and fill each half with the mushroom and feta stuffing. Cover the surface of the stuffing with a small piece of foil. Bake for 35 minutes until tender, removing the foil for the last 10 minutes of the cooking time. Serve warm with a lightly dressed mixed salad.

Somerset Chicken

You get good chickens in Somerset. This is a traditional recipe that uses two local ingredients – Cheddar cheese and cider – so we didn't mess with it. Makes a really nice supper dish, served with some baked potatoes to mop up the juices.

Serves 6
6 boneless chicken breasts, skin on
3 tbsp olive oil
75g butter
2 onions, sliced
4 tbsp plain flour
2 tbsp grain mustard
2 dessert apples, peeled and sliced into
    batons
110g button mushrooms, sliced
250ml chicken stock
300ml cider
250ml double cream
1 tbsp finely chopped sage leaves
300g Cheddar cheese, grated
6 baked potatoes

Preheat the oven to 200°C/Fan 180°C/Gas 6. Season the chicken breasts with salt and black pepper. Heat a large sauté pan and add 2 tablespoons of the oil and 50g of the butter.

Fry the chicken breasts in batches for 1–2 minutes on each side until golden. Put them into a deep-sided oven tray and roast for 25 minutes until the chicken is cooked through.

Add the remaining butter and oil to the sauté pan and cook the onions for 4–5 minutes until softened but not coloured. Add the flour and mustard to the pan and cook for another 2 minutes. Add the apples and button mushrooms and cook for 1 minute. Pour in the chicken stock and bring to the boil, then pour in the cider. Bring back to the boil and cook for 5 minutes. Add the cream and sage, cook for another 5 minutes, then season with salt and black pepper.

Take the chicken out of the oven and pour the sauce into the dish to cover the chicken completely. Preheat the grill to high. Sprinkle the cheese over the chicken and place under the grill for 5 minutes until the cheese is melted, golden and bubbling. Serve with jacket potatoes topped with a knob of butter.

Tip: Cheddar is now produced all over the world, but the cheese did originally come from the village of Cheddar in Somerset and has been made since the 12th century. Legend has it that the first Cheddar was made when a milkmaid left a pail of milk in the Cheddar Gorge caves. She came back to find it had been transformed – into cheese.

Chocolate and Orange Soufflés

The French word 'soufflé' means 'puffed up' which is exactly what a good soufflé should be. Soufflés were invented in France in the 18th century and have been a classic of French cuisine ever since. There are sweet and savoury versions, but we think you can't beat a chocolate soufflé.

Makes 6
15g butter, for greasing
Brown sugar, for sprinkling
150g dark chocolate, broken into squares
3 large egg yolks
75ml double cream
Finely grated zest of ½ small orange
2 tbsp orange liqueur, such as Cointreau
½ tsp vanilla extract
5 large egg whites
40g soft light brown sugar
Icing sugar and finely grated orange zest, to
    decorate

For the Boozy Cream

200ml double cream
2 tbsp orange liqueur, such as Cointreau
2 tbsp soft light brown sugar

Grease 6 x 175ml large ramekins or large oven-proof coffee cups with butter. Sprinkle a little brown sugar in each ramekin or cup and roll it around until the inside is lightly coated in sugar. Place the ramekins or cups on a baking tray, spaced well apart.

Put the chocolate in a heatproof bowl and set it over a pan of gently simmering water. Melt over a low heat until almost smooth, then carefully remove the bowl and stir the chocolate with a wooden spoon until smooth. Beat the 3 egg yolks into the hot melted chocolate and stir in the cream, zest, liqueur and vanilla extract. Leave to cool for 10 minutes. Preheat the oven 220°C/ Fan 200°C/Gas 7.

While the chocolate mixture is cooling, prepare the boozy cream. Put the double cream, liqueur and sugar in a mixing bowl and whip with an electric whisk until soft peaks form. Set aside.

Whisk the 5 egg whites together in a large bowl until stiff but not dry. You should be able to turn the bowl upside down without the egg whites sliding out. Add the 40g of soft brown sugar, a little at a time, whisking well in between each addition.

Fold a quarter of the egg whites into the chocolate mixture to loosen it, then fold in the rest with a metal spoon. Take care not to over stir the mixture or the eggs will lose volume. If you have some stubborn lumps of egg white, cut through the mixture a couple of times with a large metal whisk instead of folding or stirring.

Spoon the mixture into the ramekins and bake in the centre of the oven for about 9–10 minutes until well risen but with a slight wobble in the centre. Dust the tops with sifted icing sugar, place the ramekins on dessert plates and top with spoonfuls of boozy cream. Sprinkle with a little orange zest and serve immediately.

has something for everyone

Stories to make you laugh

Stories to make you feel good

Stories to take you to another place

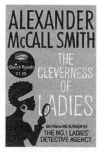

Stories about real life

Stories to take you to another time

Stories to make you turn the pages

For a complete list of titles visit
www.readingagency.org.uk/quickreads

Available in paperback, ebook and from your local library

About Quick Reads

Quick Reads are brilliant short new books written by bestselling writers. They are perfect for regular readers wanting a fast and satisfying read, but they are also ideal for adults who are discovering reading for pleasure for the first time.

Since Quick Reads was founded in 2006, over 4.5 million copies of more than a hundred titles have been sold or distributed. Quick Reads are available in paperback, in ebook and from your local library.

To find out more about Quick Reads titles, visit
www.readingagency.org.uk/quickreads
Tweet us 🐦@Quick_Reads #GalaxyQuickReads

Quick Reads is part of The Reading Agency,
a national charity that inspires more people to read more, encourages them to share their enjoyment of reading with others and celebrates the difference that reading makes to all our lives.
www.readingagency.org.uk Tweet us @readingagency

The Reading Agency Ltd • Registered number: 3904882 (England & Wales) Registered charity number: 1085443 (England & Wales) Registered Office: Free Word Centre, 60 Farringdon Road, London, EC1R 3GA The Reading Agency is supported using public funding by Arts Council England.

We would like to thank all our funders:

LOTTERY FUNDED

Discover the pleasure of reading with Galaxy®

Curled up on the sofa,
Sunday morning in pyjamas,
just before bed,
in the bath or
on the way to work?

Wherever, whenever,
you can escape
with a good book!

So go on...
indulge yourself with
a good read and the
smooth taste of
Galaxy® chocolate.

Proudly supports

Start a new chapter

On The Rock

Andy McNab

This is the call he is always ready for. They've had word of a planned attack. That's why he's back here, opposite some suit who's trying to tell him what he needs to do. But he knows exactly what's required. Four men. Plain clothes. Eyes peeled. Three targets. Two cases. One car. Gibraltar isn't an ideal location. Too many people. Too many blind alleys. But then again, he's not the terrorist. Who knows what goes through their minds? Well, he will soon. If everything goes to plan.

Available in paperback, ebook and from your local library
Corgi

Start a new chapter

I Am Malala

An abridged edition

Malala Yousafzai

with Christina Lamb

When the Taliban took control of the Swat Valley,
one girl fought for her right to an education.
On Tuesday 9 October 2012, she almost paid the ultimate
price when she was shot in the head at point-blank range.

Malala Yousafzai's extraordinary journey has taken her from
a remote valley in northern Pakistan to the halls of the United
Nations. She has become a global symbol of peaceful protest
and is the youngest ever winner of the Nobel Peace Prize.

I Am Malala will make you believe in the power of
one person's voice to inspire change in the world.

Available in paperback, ebook and from your local library

Weidenfeld & Nicolson

Start a new chapter

A Baby at the Beach Café

Lucy Diamond

Evie loves running her beach café in Cornwall but with
a baby on the way, she's been told to put her feet up.
Let someone else take over? Not likely.

Helen's come to Cornwall to escape the stress
of city living. She hopes a seaside life will be the answer
to all her dreams. When she sees a job advertised
at the café it sounds perfect.

But the two women clash and sparks fly . . .
and then events take a dramatic turn. Can the pair
of them put aside their differences in a crisis?

Why not start a reading group?

If you have enjoyed this book, why not share your next Quick Read with friends, colleagues, or neighbours?

The Reading Agency also runs **Reading Groups for Everyone** which helps you discover and share new books. Find a reading group near you, or register a group you already belong to and get free books and offers from publishers at **readinggroups.org**

A reading group is a great way to get the most out of a book and is easy to arrange. All you need is a group of people, a place to meet and a date and time that works for everyone.

Use the first meeting to decide which book to read first and how the group will operate. Conversation doesn't have to stick rigidly to the book. Here are some suggested themes for discussions:

- How important was the plot?
- What messages are in the book?
- Discuss the characters – were they believable and could you relate to them?
- How important was the setting to the story?
- Are the themes timeless?
- Personal reactions – what did you like or not like about the book?

There is a free toolkit with lots of ideas to help you run a Quick Reads reading group at **www.readingagency.org.uk/quickreads**

Share your experiences of your group on Twitter @Quick_Reads #GalaxyQuickReads

Continuing your reading journey

As well as Quick Reads, The Reading Agency runs lots of programmes to help keep you reading.

Reading Ahead invites you to pick six reads and record your reading in a diary in order to get a certificate. If you're thinking about improving your reading or would like to read more, then this is for you. Find out more at **www.readingahead.org.uk**

World Book Night is an annual celebration of reading and books on 23 April, which sees passionate volunteers give out books in their communities to share their love of reading. Find out more at **worldbooknight.org**

Reading together with a child will help them to develop a lifelong love of reading. Our **Chatterbooks** children's reading groups and **Summer Reading Challenge** inspire children to read more and share the books they love. Find out more at **readingagency.org.uk/children**

Find more books for new readers at

- **www.readingahead.org.uk/find-a-read**
- **www.newisland.ie**
- **www.barringtonstoke.co.uk**